"I would like you to stay until Gideon is better," Becca said.

"But you must understand that we cannot afford to pay you for your help."

Tully leaned back in his chair. A wry smile curved his lips and showed a dimple in his right cheek. "A few days of your good cooking will be payment enough. You don't have to worry about putting me up. I can sleep in the barn if the animals don't mind my snoring."

"Why are you doing this?"

His smile disappeared. His eyes grew serious. He leaned forward and clasped his hands together on the tabletop. "I wasn't exaggerating when I said it had been a long time since I was somewhere that felt like a home. When I got out of the army two years ago, things didn't go well for me. Let's just say I messed up. Somebody gave me a helping hand when I needed it. I'd like to think I'm repaying that favor by helping you and your family. Just until Gideon is back on his feet."

After thirty-five years as a nurse, **Patricia Davids** hung up her stethoscope to become a full-time writer. She enjoys spending her free time visiting her grandchildren, doing some long-overdue yard work and traveling to research her story locations. She resides in Wichita, Kansas. Pat always enjoys hearing from her readers. You can visit her online at patriciadavids.com.

Books by Patricia Davids

Love Inspired

North Country Amish

An Amish Wife for Christmas
Shelter from the Storm
The Amish Teacher's Dilemma
A Haven for Christmas

The Amish Bachelors

An Amish Harvest
An Amish Noel
His Amish Teacher
Their Pretend Amish Courtship
Amish Christmas Twins
An Unexpected Amish Romance
His New Amish Family

HQN Books

The Amish of Cedar Grove

The Wish
The Hope
The Prayer

Visit the Author Profile page at Harlequin.com for more titles.

A Haven
for Christmas

Patricia Davids

LOVE INSPIRED
INSPIRATIONAL ROMANCE

LOVE INSPIRED®

INSPIRATIONAL ROMANCE

Recycling programs
for this product may
not exist in your area.

ISBN-13: 978-1-335-48847-3

A Haven for Christmas

Copyright © 2020 by Patricia MacDonald

This edition published by arrangement with Harlequin Books S.A.

For questions and comments about the quality of this book,
please contact us at CustomerService@Harlequin.com.

Love Inspired
22 Adelaide St. West, 40th Floor
Toronto, Ontario M5H 4E3, Canada
www.Harlequin.com

Printed in U.S.A.

Now the God of hope fill you with all joy and peace in believing, that ye may abound in hope, through the power of the Holy Ghost.
—*Romans* 15:13

This book is dedicated to the thousands of men and women who suffer from addiction and are working to overcome it. May you find strength, solace and peace in God's love.

Chapter One

"Did Rosie have her *bobbli* last night?"

Becca Beachy pinned her daughter's white *kapp* to her thick red hair, then tweaked the seven-year-old's nose. "*Nee*, she did not. Do you think I would keep it a secret if your new calf had arrived?"

Annabeth couldn't hide her disappointment. "*Daadi* thought she might, and he knows everything about cows."

Becca glanced over her daughter's head to where her father-in-law sat at the kitchen table enjoying his first cup of coffee. She met his eyes and arched her brow. "Your grandpa Gideon may think he knows everything about cows, but he doesn't know everything about Rosie. She will have her calf when she is ready. Not before. Sit down and eat your breakfast."

Annabeth's lower lip stuck out. "But I wanted to tell everyone at school about my new calf."

Becca gave her a small push toward the table. "When you have a new calf, you may share the story with your friends. Your impatience won't hurry the event."

Gideon coughed and put down his cup. "It might

be that your calf will be here when you get home from school today."

"Then I will have to wait until Monday to tell everyone." Annabeth plunked herself in her chair at the table with a pout on her face. She pulled her lower lip in when she caught her mother's frown and folded her hands waiting for grace to be said.

Becca dished up the scrambled eggs, sausage links and pancakes onto a plate and sat at the foot of the table. Gideon bowed his head and began the silent blessing. Becca added a plea for his improved health to her prayer of thankfulness for God's blessings. She needed his help to run the dairy. She couldn't do it alone. The last thing she wanted to face was failing at this new endeavor and having to uproot her daughter yet again. Her husband had never found the place where he wanted to put down roots. They had moved every year of their marriage, even after Annabeth was born, but Becca knew home wasn't a place to be found. It was a place to be made. Here in the north of Maine was where Becca was making a home.

When Gideon looked up, signaling the end of the prayer, Annabeth reached for the pancakes. Becca pushed the pitcher of syrup toward her, knowing her daughter's sweet tooth. She covertly studied Gideon's drawn features as they ate. He wasn't getting better, and that worried her. A cold was one thing, but his cough had hung on much longer than it should. She waited until he finished eating. "Gideon, why don't you drive Annabeth to school today? I'll take care of the milk for a change." She held her breath, waiting for his answer.

"You won't try to lift those heavy milk cans by yourself?"

Because their Amish religion didn't allow the use of electricity, their cows were milked by hand. The milk was strained and poured into ten-gallon stainless steel milk cans. The cans were taken by wagon every morning and every night to the refrigeration facility two miles away. Ten gallons of milk in a steel can weighed nearly a hundred pounds. She had filled five of them that morning. They were still sitting in the milking parlor.

She sought to ease Gideon's mind and convince him to take the easier task of driving Annabeth to their Amish school in New Covenant. "I'll wait on you and get started on my baking. If you don't stop to gossip with the neighbors, we can get the milk to the collection point before the truck comes. If we miss it, nothing is lost. The milk won't spoil in this weather. We'll take a double load this evening."

"*Nee*, you take the child. I will see to the milk as usual."

"I want you to take me. Please, *Daadi*," Annabeth said with her mouth still full of her last bite of sausage.

Becca didn't scold her for her table manners. She hoped the child's pleading would sway Gideon. It usually did. This morning was no exception. He smiled and nodded. "All right, I'll take you. It will make a nice change for your mother."

Becca's tense shoulders relaxed. "*Goot*, now take the plates to the sink, Annabeth, and go wash your hands and face."

"*Daadi*, will you tell me another story about the little boys with red hair that you used to know?" the child asked as she gathered the plates.

"If you do as your mother tells you," he said softly.

"Okay." She put the dishes in the sink and ran to wash up.

He looked at Becca. "Do you think she knows they are stories about her father and his brother?"

Becca's heart contracted with pain. "Not yet, but one day she will realize the truth and thank you for it."

Among the Amish it was proper to grieve for a lost loved one, as Becca still grieved for her husband, but it wasn't considered proper to speak about them afterward. In doing so it might appear that a person was questioning God's will in calling their loved one home. Annabeth had only the vaguest memories of her father. He died when she was barely four. Gideon's stories of the little red-haired boys were his way of sharing his memories of his sons with her without naming them.

Annabeth came rushing back into the room, pulling on her coat. "I'm ready."

Becca handed her a blue plastic lunch box and held open the door for the pair. The cold late-November air rushed in. Gideon took Annabeth's hand and walked with her to the black buggy parked by the front gate. Cider, their buggy horse, stood waiting patiently, his warm breath rising in puffs of white mist from his nostrils.

Annabeth looked up at her grandfather. "Tell me the story about how the oldest red-haired boy saved his little brother in a runaway buggy."

"You have heard it many times."

"But it's my favorite."

Gideon coughed and pressed a hand to his chest for a moment before he lifted her into the buggy. "All right. I will tell it again."

"And many more times, I pray," Becca said softly. She watched them drive away and closed the door against the chill.

* * *

"I'm sorry to do this to you, Tully. I hope you know that."

Tully Lange stared at the eviction notice he had just been handed by the kid who managed the apartment building. His rent was two weeks past due, but he had hoped to get a month's extension. So much for hope.

Things weren't going his way. He'd lost his job as a night watchman on Monday when the owner of the corner pawnshop where he worked died. Tully hadn't found another job yet, but he was looking. The high point of his week had been a lukewarm Thanksgiving dinner at the local soup kitchen the day before yesterday. And now this. Happy holidays. It was enough to drive a sober man to drink.

He crumpled the paper in his hand. He wasn't going to be that man ever again. "It's okay, Reggie. I know you're just doing your job."

The skinny young man with spiked blond hair and thick glasses sagged with relief. "It's nothing personal. You know that. The super won't let me cut you any slack. I mean, I told him you just got out of rehab. I don't think he has any idea how tough that is. Don't let this bounce you off the wagon, Tully. I've seen how hard it is to quit drinking. My brother went through rehab. It was rough, but he stayed sober seven years."

"Tell me he is still sober." At the moment Tully needed to hear it could be done.

Reggie pressed his lips together and stared at his feet. "I wish I could. His wife left him. He couldn't handle it. But hey, seven years, that's a lot."

Tully turned away before Reggie could see how crushed he was. For every story about people who stayed sober, there were dozens more about people who had failed. "Yeah, seven years is a lot. I hope he finds his way back to sobriety."

"Thanks, man. I hope he does, too. What are you going to do?"

"I've got no job. It looks like I've only got two weeks left in this paradise." He let his gaze drift over the peeling paint, tattered carpet and water-stained ceiling in what passed for a lobby of the low-rent Philadelphia apartment complex the rehab center had located for him. What was he going to do? "I'll think of something."

"I can let you know if I hear about a job." The offer was half-hearted, but Tully nodded his thanks.

Too bad his Alcoholics Anonymous meeting wasn't tonight. He could still call his sponsor and…do what? Cry on the man's shoulder? Life was tough. Tully Lange, formerly Sergeant Lange of the United States Army, needed to be tougher.

At least no one was shooting at him.

He unlocked his mailbox and pulled out the usual junk mail along with one oversize red envelope. He smiled when he saw it was from Arnie Dawson, also formerly of the United States Army and a longtime friend. Arnie was among the few people Tully had told he was going into rehab.

He tore open the envelope. On the front of the card inside was a baby in a diaper wearing a black mortarboard cap with a gold tassel. Inside the card read, "Graduation is only the first step. Keep stepping."

Arnie had added a handwritten note.

Couldn't find a card that said "congrats on getting through rehab." Thought this one had pretty much the same message. I'm real proud of you,

*Cowboy. I wish I had half your guts. Pop up to
Maine and see me soon. We'll swap lies about
our good old army days. I might even convince
an Okie like you to stay in my slice of heaven.*

Arnie loved teasing Tully about his Oklahoma roots,
boots and Midwestern drawl. He never called Tully anything except Cowboy. Tully turned the envelope over
and studied the return address. Caribou, Maine. The
place even sounded cold. Would there be snow already?
Tully almost chuckled. Wouldn't Arnie be shocked if
he took him up on his offer?

"Well, why not?" he muttered to himself. What did
he have to lose?

"Why not what?" Reggie asked.

Tully had forgotten the boy was still hovering nearby.
"A buddy has invited me to visit him in Maine. I guess
I've got the time. It'll be good to see him again."

"Maine? Nothing but lumberjacks and moose that far
north, unless he lives on the coast. I hear the seafood is
awesome, though. At least that's what they say on those
TV travel channels. I've never been there myself. I've
never been outside Philadelphia."

Tully stared at the envelope in his hand. If he spent
the rest of his last paycheck on gas, he could make it
in a day or two, provided his car had that many more
miles left in it. He didn't have much to pack. That was
the upside of being homeless and living out of his car
for a year. The only upside.

An unfamiliar sense of excitement began creeping in
to replace the despair that always hovered at the edge of
his consciousness. A road trip and a visit with a friend
he hadn't seen in more than two years. What better way

to celebrate four months of sobriety and the upcoming Christmas season? He needed to go. He had to get away before his old life pulled him back down to the gutter. Maybe this was his chance to make a real change.

He tossed the junk mail in the trash can by the door and walked down the musty-smelling hall to his studio apartment. He would let his sponsor know where he was going so he didn't think Tully had relapsed. Other than his outpatient therapist, there was no one else to tell now that his old boss was gone.

He had burned a lot of bridges with the people in his life. This was his chance to save one of the few he had left.

Now that he had a plan, he rushed to get going before he changed his mind. Before he didn't make it past the bar on Clover Street.

How many times had his determination to get sober been derailed in the past? There had always been a bar or a liquor store between him and his commitment to quit drinking. There would be one in Caribou, Maine, too. But there would also be his friend Arnie and most likely an AA group nearby if he needed help.

He pulled himself up short. Not if. He would need help. It would never be easy.

If he had learned anything in rehab, it was that his alcoholism could be mastered but never cured.

Now that the first rush of enthusiasm was wearing off, Tully sat on the worn, lumpy gray sofa that served as his couch and bed. He pulled out his cell phone, grateful that the rehab facility had provided him with a prepaid one. It didn't have any bells and whistles, but a fellow couldn't get a job without a phone and an address. He punched in Arnie's number. His buddy picked up on the third ring.

"What did you think of the card?"

Not even a hello. Tully chuckled. "I think your taste is questionable."

"Give me the spiel."

Tully knew what he meant. It was the way AA members introduced themselves at his local meeting. "Hello. My name is Tully and I'm an alcoholic. I've been sober for four months and five days."

"Man, you don't know how good it is to hear from you, Cowboy. Have you heard from any of the other guys?" Arnie asked hopefully.

"I heard Mason reenlisted but only because O'Connor stopped by to visit me once in rehab. He didn't know where anyone else was, but he had heard about Brian." Saying his friend's name still choked him. He drew a shaky breath.

"It wasn't your fault," Arnie said firmly.

How Tully wished that was true. "I knew how drunk Brian was. I had his car keys. Why did I give them back to him?"

It had been the last straw. The last bad decision that cost his friend his life and the lives of two other people when Brian ran a red light. It had been rock bottom for Tully. It had been his wake-up call.

"You handed over the keys because you were drunk, too. You weren't thinking straight."

It was an easy excuse. One that he would never use again.

"You can't change the past, buddy," Arnie said.

"I know."

"Have you found a new job?"

"Not yet. I've been looking. I need to find one person to have faith in me and believe I'll stay sober. There don't seem to be many like that around here. The truth is, I'm on my way to see you."

"What? You're coming here? When?" Arnie's surprised excitement was what Tully hoped to hear.

"When? That depends. How long does it take to drive from Philadelphia to Reindeer?"

"Caribou."

"Right. Same thing." Tully knew his friend wouldn't let that slide.

"Caribou are not reindeer, my cowboy friend. While they may be the same species, reindeer have been domesticated for more than two thousand years. Caribou are wild. It's sort of like comparing a mustang to a Shetland pony."

Tully laughed. He should've called Arnie ages ago. "My grandpa bought a Shetland pony for us kids. That animal put any mustang to shame when it came to bucking off a rider. Billy was the meanest little horse that ever walked the earth."

"I've missed your Oklahoma ranch life stories."

"Look, I have to be stingy with my minutes. How long?"

"Twelve hours if you go straight through, but don't. You don't want to meet a moose when you're sleepy."

"Okay. You'll see me when you see me, and I will avoid meeting any and all moose." Tully hung up and sat back. This was a good decision. At least he hoped it was.

Fourteen hours later, dawn was only a faint light in the eastern sky when Tully rounded a bend on an isolated snow-covered stretch of Maine highway. That wasn't a moose in his headlights. It was a Holstein cow. He hit his brakes and swerved to miss her. He didn't see the calf until it was too late.

* * *

"Can I help you milk this morning?" Annabeth asked, rubbing the sleep from her eyes as she came into the kitchen.

"You just want to check on Rosie. I'll come and get you if she has had her calf." Becca glanced at Gideon's door. He wasn't up yet. She didn't intend to wake him. It was Sunday, but there was no church service this week. It was a day of rest, and Gideon needed it. Hopefully she would have most of the milking done before he joined her.

She finished washing the milk pails and gathered the handles of two in each hand. "Open the door for me, daughter."

Annabeth pulled the kitchen door open and took a step back. "*Mamm*, there's a man stealing Rosie. He has a calf, too!"

Becca moved to stand behind her daughter. There was a stranger outside their front gate. It wasn't one of their Amish neighbors or anyone else she knew. He was *Englisch* by his dress. He was wearing jeans, a faded blue denim jacket and a battered gray cowboy hat. He didn't seem intent on fleeing with his armload of newborn calf. Rosie stood beside him, nosing the baby's face and licking her.

"I don't think he is stealing our cow, but I have no idea what he is doing."

She stepped outside the screen door and put her buckets on the porch floor. "Can we help you?"

"Ma'am, is this your cow?" His slow drawl was low and husky.

"That's my Rosie," Annabeth said peering around Becca.

"You have a new little heifer, but she is hurt. Where should I put her?"

Becca spoke quietly to her daughter in Pennsylvania Dutch, the language the Amish spoke at home. "Go wake your grandpa."

Annabeth darted down the hallway. Becca then walked down the steps of the porch and stopped with her hands on the gate. "Where did you find her?"

He gestured toward the cow with his head. "Mama was standing in the middle of the highway about a quarter mile from here. Her calf was off to the side of the road. I swerved to miss the cow and hit the calf. She's scraped up, and her front leg is broken. I'm real sorry, ma'am."

The loss of any animal was hard to bear, but Annabeth was going to be heartbroken if the calf couldn't be saved. "Bring her down to the barn."

Becca hurried ahead of him and was surprised to see the corral gate standing wide-open. She quickly closed it and held open the barn door for him. "That would explain how Rosie got out." How many others had found the opening?

The man followed her inside the barn. "I once had a horse that could open a barn door by himself. He just took the handle in his teeth and turned his head, but I've never heard of a cow doing it."

"I suspect my daughter left it unlatched when she came out to check on Rosie last night. She has been waiting eagerly for this calf to arrive."

"You might want to check the rest of your cattle. I saw a lot of tracks heading out your lane."

"I was just thinking that." She opened a stall door. He carried the calf inside and tenderly laid her down. She struggled to get up. He kept her down with one hand. "Easy, little one. You just take it easy. Every-thing's gonna be okay." The calf quieted at his gentle reassurances. "You might want to close that gate so Mama doesn't get in here with us."

It took a second for Becca to realize he was speaking to her in the same soothing tone. She quickly shut the stall door. Rosie tried to push her way in, but to no avail.

The first rays of the sun streamed through the small window and illuminated the pen. He pushed back the brim of his hat, and she got her first good look at the calf's rescuer. His eyes as he gazed up at her were such a deep brown they almost looked black. His hair—what she could see of it—was black as a crow's wing and cut short as a newly shorn sheep. His face was thin, as if he had recently lost weight. Her guess was borne out by the extra notches she noticed beside the silver buckle in the tooled leather belt he wore to hold up his loose jeans. He had on boots, but not the kind she was used to seeing. The pointed toes didn't look comfortable, but they were clearly well-worn. He didn't say anything. He just waited for her to finish her assessment.

"Thank you for stopping to care for my animals. I am Rebecca Beachy, but everyone calls me Becca."

He touched the brim of his hat. "Pleased to meet you. My name is Tully—"

She saw a flash of indecision in his eyes before his gaze fell away from hers. He turned back to the calf. "I can splint this leg until your veterinarian can get out here."

His quick change of topic had her wondering what else he had meant to say but didn't.

Chapter Two

Tully kept his gaze on the injured calf. He couldn't believe he'd almost introduced himself to this pretty Amish woman as an alcoholic. He was still embarrassed to admit that he was one, even though he knew accepting it was part of the process of coming to grips with his addiction, but it didn't feel right to tell her. She'd probably never dealt with a drunk in her life. He prayed she never would.

"What is this my granddaughter tells me? Has someone come to steal our *milch kuh*? Seems to me he should take her out of the barn, not bring her inside. But perhaps he's not a very good thief."

Tully glanced up to see a formidable-looking Amish man scowling at him from beside Rosie. The little red-headed girl he had seen earlier was peeking from behind him through the wooden slats of the gate. She and her mother shared the same intense green eyes. Where the child had bright red hair, her mother's was a deep auburn.

"Annabeth, you know that's not the truth," Becca said. "Gideon, this is Tully. Tully, this is my father-in-law,

Gideon Beachy. Tully found Rosie and her calf out on the highway. He accidentally struck the calf with his car. She's hurt."

Gideon looked down at the child. "And how did Rosie find her way out to the highway?"

"I don't know," Annabeth said, trying hard to look like an innocent little girl. Tully struggled not to smile.

"Someone did not latch the gate properly when she came out to check on Rosie last night," Becca suggested with a pointed look at the child.

"I thought I latched it."

"Next time you will make sure." Her grandfather's stern tone caused the little one to nod and bow her head. He spoke with a thick accent that reminded Tully of the time he had been stationed in Germany. "Now we will see what must be done to help Rosie's baby."

Gideon pushed the big cow away from the gate and slipped inside. Annabeth climbed to the top and looked on.

"The right foreleg is broken," Tully said. "We should splint it until your veterinarian can examine her. I'm more concerned about her head. She seems pretty groggy."

He caught the look that passed between Gideon and Becca. He wasn't sure if the Amish used veterinarians. Maybe they would just put her down to keep her from suffering. "A simple break in a calf this young will heal fine if it's properly splinted and you can keep her from moving around too much."

Gideon nodded at Becca. "Go to the phone shack and call Doc Pike."

"Can we afford that?"

"We'll manage."

Tully wished he could offer to pay for the vet, but he had less than twenty dollars to his name.

"I will see if I can find something to make a splint." Becca left the stall and took Annabeth with her.

Gideon sank down beside the calf, keeping one leg extended in an awkward position. He patted his thigh. "I know something about broken bones. Let us see if she has other injuries."

The two men carefully examined the calf. "She seems okay," Tully said.

"You know something about cattle?" Gideon asked.

"Beef cattle. Angus, mostly. I grew up on a ranch in Oklahoma. I know next to nothing about dairy cattle except that your Holsteins are really big."

Gideon chuckled. "I have thought the same thing when one is standing on my foot."

"I noticed tracks in the snow leading away from the house. Any idea how many more cattle are missing?"

"It can't be many. I saw at least six waiting to be milked. We have eleven counting Rosie. I will check as soon as we take care of this one. A man can solve only one problem at a time, no matter how much he wants to do everything at once."

Tully smiled. "I like your philosophy."

Becca came back into the barn a short time later with several rolls of cloth tucked under her arm. She held a length of plastic pipe in her hand. "Doc Pike says he'll be here in an hour. Will this work to stabilize the leg if you cut it in half lengthwise? It was left over from when we put in the new water system."

Gideon got up and took the pipe from her. "It should. I'll be back in a bit."

Tully held the calf's leg straight, making it bawl in

protest. "Go ahead and pad it before we put the splint over it."

She had to lean close to him in order to bind the leg. She spoke gently to the calf with the same singsong German accent as Gideon. Her hands were small compared to Tully's, deft and gentle as she worked. Her auburn hair was parted in the middle and tucked beneath a white bonnet. He wasn't sure if it was her hair or bonnet that smelled fresh, like linen that had been dried in the sun. It reminded him of the way his grandmother's sheets used to smell when he had helped her gather them off the clothesline. It was a good memory. One that had been buried far too long beneath unhappy, painful ones.

It had been a while since he had spent time this close to a woman. "Your hair smells nice. Like sunshine."

She drew back. Her startled, wide-eyed expression told him he'd said something wrong. "I'm sorry. I meant that as a compliment."

She went back to work. "To say such things is not our way."

"Then I apologize. I meant no disrespect. I don't need an irate Amish husband coming after me."

She smoothed the end of the bandage into place. "My husband is dead, so you need not fear." She got to her feet and left without looking at him.

He closed his eyes and hung his head. "Nice going, Tully. Insult the first Amish lady you've ever met. Maybe keep your mouth shut from now on."

"Even a fool is counted wise if he says nothing," Gideon said as he came in with the cut piece of pipe in his hand.

Tully nodded. "Good advice given five minutes too late. I regret that I upset your daughter-in-law by mentioning her husband, your son, and I'm sorry for your loss."

"It was *Gott*'s will. My son is at peace. You had no way of knowing. Becca will not hold your words against you. For us forgiveness comes first." Gideon handed Tully the length of pipe. "See if this fits our patient's leg."

It did, and they used the rest of the cloth strips to secure it in place over the padding.

Rosie had been standing quietly outside the gate, but now she gave a low moo. The calf bawled pitifully.

Tully got up. "Maybe she's getting hungry. Let's see if she can stand."

He lifted the little heifer to her feet. She wobbled but couldn't stay upright without Tully holding her.

Gideon grimaced. "*Dat es* not *goot*."

"Let Mama in and see what she does." Tully hated to get his hopes up. He wasn't used to having things work out for the best, but the little critter deserved a chance. Gideon opened the stall. Rosie came in and began to lick her baby. The calf made no effort to stand. Tully lifted her and positioned her at her mother's udder. With a little coaxing, he was able to get her to latch on and suckle, but she gave up after only a few minutes. Tully lowered her to the floor. It wasn't looking good.

"My granddaughter will gladly bottle-feed her. She feels bad about leaving the gate unlatched." Gideon started coughing and struggled to catch his breath.

Tully shot a sharp glance at the older man. "Are you okay?"

Gideon nodded. After a minute he cleared his throat. "I will be fine. I must go get the rest of my cows before the lumber trucks start coming down the highway. They don't slow down for anything smaller than another truck."

"I'll go round up your cattle. That's what cowboys do."

"Are you truly a cowboy like those from the wild West?" Gideon looked intrigued.

"Among other things."

Tully didn't bother to list the jobs he'd had and failed at since leaving the ranch at seventeen. The only place he'd truly fit in had been the army. He missed the camaraderie of his unit and the sense of belonging that had once bound them together. Loyalty to the men he'd fought beside had carried him through two tours of duty in some mean places, where losing those same friends came with a high cost. After a while it became easier not to have friends or to be one. The bottle had helped with that until it became his only friend.

He walked out of the barn into the sunshine of a new morning and drew a deep breath. Those days were behind him. He was sober. He was going to stay that way.

Becca walked toward him, carrying four shiny buckets. He gestured toward the lane. "I'm going to get the rest of your gals."

"Let me give these to Gideon so he can start milking and I'll help you."

He knew he could probably manage by himself, but he waited anyway. She came hurrying out of the barn a few moments later. "We are missing four."

Together they walked quickly to the end of the lane. She saw the tracks without him pointing them out. It was no surprise. She was a country girl used to being around cattle. She could probably track them better than he could.

She put her hand to her brow to block the bright sunlight glaring off the snow as she scanned the area to the east. "It looks like they are headed toward New Covenant. There's no telling how far they could've gotten."

"Why don't we take my car? We can use it to herd them back. I'd much rather use a good cowpony, but I can make do with a beat-up Ford."

She hesitated but then nodded.

"Wait here. I'll get it." He started jogging up the roadway to where he had been stopped by Rosie.

Becca didn't seem to be upset with him for his careless remark about her deceased husband. That was good. If he could get her cattle rounded up, it would even the score in his eyes. He reached his car and looked back. She was nowhere in sight.

A sharp stab of disappointment hit him. She must have decided she didn't want to ride with him after all. He couldn't blame her. He was a stranger. Not many women would willingly hop in a car with someone they didn't know. He got in, turned around and drove past her lane in the direction the cattle had gone. He rounded a shallow curve in the road and saw her walking with her head down. He pulled to a stop beside her and pushed open the passenger side door.

Becca had prayed that her cows would be just around the bend, but they weren't. She faced Tully in his car. She wasn't afraid of him, but she found him…disturbing. She was curious about him, and that was unusual. She rarely gave a stranger a second thought, especially an *Englisch* stranger, but there was something about this kindhearted man that appealed to her. She liked him.

That alone should be enough to make her refuse

his offer of a ride. Instead she got in the front seat beside him.

"You won't get in trouble for riding in a car, will you? I know the Amish use horses and buggies. I wouldn't want to get you shunned or whatever it is you call it."

She looked straight ahead. "Riding in a car is permitted. Owning one is not. To be shunned I would have to deliberately disobey the rules of my church. Shunning is a very serious matter and is never done lightly."

"Now I'm just feeling ignorant. I confess I know nothing about you folks."

She looked at him then. "You cannot be expected to know our ways. I appreciate your concern for me."

"Okay, since I don't have to worry about getting you in trouble, where do you think your cows might've gone?" He drove slowly, scanning both sides of the highway for any sign of the animals.

"Their tracks ended where they started walking on the highway. I was hoping they were in the neighbor's field, but something must have tempted them to move farther along."

"Who else has cattle near this road? I've never met a cow that didn't want to investigate another herd."

"We are the only dairy, but nearly all of our neighbors have at least one milk cow."

They came to an intersection. He stopped the car and got out. She bent her head to see him. "What are you doing?"

"I'm listening. I hear bellowing coming from that direction." He walked away from the car and examined the ground beside the road for a dozen yards. He gave her a thumbs-up sign and came jogging back. He climbed in and flashed her a boyish grin. "They went that way. A couple of them stepped off the roadway and left tracks."

They drove on until she spotted her four cows standing by a pasture fence where a dozen young steers were bawling at them.

Tully stopped the car. "Do those animals look familiar?"

"They look like Bessy, Flo, Dotty and Maude."

"Then let's see if we can convince them to leave their newfound babies. Those youngsters don't sound like they have been weaned very long by the way they are calling for their mamas." He cupped his hands around his mouth and gave a loud imitation of a bawling calf.

She grinned. "That's *goot*. Perhaps they will follow you if you talk to them sweetly."

"Ya think?" His dark eyes sparkled with mirth.

"I think it will take more persuasion." She got out of the car and walked toward the cattle.

Tully got out, too, circled around to the other side of them and raised his arms. "Ha, cow, ha. Move out. Let's go."

The group reluctantly left the fence and ambled toward the road as he encouraged them. It seemed they had tired of their adventure and were ready to go home and be milked. Once they were headed in the right direction, Becca walked behind them urging them along. Tully got back in his car and followed her with his flashers on to warn anyone coming up behind them.

He rolled down his window as he came up even with her. "I wish there was a way to get around them and make sure they turn the right direction at the intersection. Is there another road I can take?"

"*Nee*, there is not. They will go the right way."

"What makes you so sure?"

"Because I see one of our neighbors coming this way. He will lend us a helping hand." Up ahead she saw Michael Shetler wave at her from his buggy. She waved back.

He leaned out the window. "Are you driving them home?" he shouted.

"*Ja*, will you make sure they go the right way at the crossroads?" she yelled back.

"I will." He turned his buggy around and returned to the intersection to wait for them.

She looked at Tully. "We can manage them from here."

"Is that your way of saying 'get lost, Cowboy'?"

Before she could answer, one of the cows spun around and made a dash past her, galloping toward the calves still bawling in the distance.

"I'll get her." Tully put his car in Reverse and shot backward until he was ahead of the animal. He got out and raised his arms. "Whoa. Wrong way, darlin'."

Dotty stopped and lowered her head. Becca held her breath, afraid the big cow was going to charge him. The most obstinate one in the herd, Dotty could easily knock him aside. His confidence seemed to deter her, but only for a moment. She charged. He jumped out of her way. She went by him without pausing.

Tully dashed back to his car and overtook the cow once again. This time he used his car to block her path as he laid on the horn. She gave up and went trotting back to the group.

Tully pulled up beside Becca once more with a big grin on his face. "Now what were you saying?"

He was enjoying teasing her. She tipped her head in

resignation. "I was thinking perhaps you should follow us all the way home to prevent any more breakaways."

"That's what I thought you would be thinking."

Dotty stopped in the road and looked back. He honked his horn, and she kept walking. He held his arms wide. "See. I'm useful."

Becca smiled to herself as she walked on. He was much too charming for her peace of mind, but she was glad for the help and would find a way to repay him.

The cattle turned the right way at the intersection with Michael working as a blocker. Once the cattle were ambling toward her home, Tully rolled down the window of his car and doffed his hat to Michael. "Thanks for the help."

Michael was leaning out the window of his buggy. "Have you hired a cowboy to manage your herd now, Becca?" he asked with a chuckle.

"*Nee*, this is Tully Lange, who stopped to lend a hand." She didn't bother explaining how they had met. The cows were getting farther away from her.

"We are grateful for your kindness," Michael said.

"I hope they don't go past the lane. *Danki*, Michael." She hurried after her cows, but they were done wandering and turned toward home as if that had been their plan all along. Gideon held the corral gate open, and they filed into the corral and into the barn to be milked.

Annabeth was waiting for Becca on the front porch. "I'm sorry I let the cows out, *Mamm*."

"You are forgiven. I hope you have learned something."

"Not to be in a rush when I close the gate."

Becca patted her daughter's head. "Life gives the test first and then teaches you the lesson afterward."

"Doc Pike is here. He is going to put a cast on the calf's leg."

"Okay. Go on inside. Set the table for breakfast while I finish helping Gideon with the milking."

"Is that man going to eat with us?"

"Tully? I think that's a *goot* idea. It's the least we can do after all his help. He was kind to carry Rosie's baby home to us, don't you think?"

"I guess. Can I name the baby?"

"Of course. You have named all the others. Do you have one in mind?"

"I'll ponder it for a while." She rubbed her chin the way Gideon did when he was giving something extra thought.

Becca held back a grin and went into the barn. Gideon stood with Tully watching the vet work. After finishing the cast, the vet stood and shook his head. "I'm worried that she isn't more active. Let's let her rest for now. I've given her something for the pain. Hopefully she'll perk up soon. When she does, try to get some milk into her. If she'll stand, put her with her mother every three or four hours, but it's probably safest to keep them separated the rest of the time until the calf is more active. You can try bottle-feeding if she won't nurse. I'll check back with you folks tomorrow." He gathered up his supplies and left.

Becca turned to Tully. "Are you leaving us now, too?" For some reason she was reluctant to say goodbye.

Chapter Three

Tully touched the brim of his hat. "If it's all the same, I'd like to stick around for a while and see how she gets on."

"I'm sure that's fine." Becca glanced at Gideon. He nodded.

Tully smiled at her. "Thanks. I feel responsible for causing you folks so much trouble. As soon as I get a job, I'll repay you for the vet bill."

"That won't be necessary," Gideon said.

"All the same, that's what I intend to do."

"Breakfast will be ready soon. I hope you will join us," Becca said.

He started to refuse, but something in her eyes made him change his mind. "Breakfast sounds great. Thanks."

Becca grinned happily. "*Goot.* I will start cooking once we finish milking."

Gideon looked from Becca to Tully and back. "Tully will help me finish. He has been telling me he wants to learn to milk a cow."

"That's right, I do," Tully said, although this was the first that it had been mentioned. "A man can't really consider his education complete until he's milked at least one cow."

"Are you sure?" She was looking at Gideon.

"Go cook and leave this work to the men." Gideon dismissed her with a wave of his hand. She looked ready to argue but held her peace.

Tully watched her leave the barn. Gideon clapped a hand on his shoulder. "Come, I will show you what to do."

"That's good, because I'm pretty much clueless. We got our milk from the grocery store in town."

"They charge too much." He walked to the first cow who was standing in her stanchion patiently waiting. He took a three-legged stool off the wall and showed Tully how to place it beside the cow and sit down.

The first thing Tully noticed was that his hat was in the way. He pulled it off and looked for a place to put it. Gideon chuckled. "Not a milking hat?"

"Nope, but I'm partial to it." It was a reminder that he'd once had the right to call himself a cowboy. That ranch life and the open prairie were part of his DNA. Although that life was in the distant past, it would forever be a part of him. He handed his hat to Gideon, who hung it on a wooden peg on the wall along with his own.

He took a flat brimless hat off the wall and clapped it on his head. It was Tully's turn to laugh. "All you need is a red jacket and a hand organ."

"Are you saying I look like a monkey in my milking hat?"

"There is a vague resemblance."

"We will see who is the monkey when you can't fill your pail."

Gideon showed Tully how to brush the cow's back

legs, tail and udder to prevent any debris from dropping into the pail. Then he showed him how to wash and dry the teats. He stood behind Tully, giving him a few directions on how best to go about milking without hurting the cow before he moved to the adjacent animal and set to work.

It didn't take Tully long to get the rhythm. He was nowhere near as fast as Gideon, but he filled his bucket before the older man had filled his second one. Tully moved to the next cow. The muscles in his forearms were burning before he was done with her.

"Not bad for an *Englischer*." Gideon stroked his long beard.

Tully glanced up at him. "What's an *Englischer*?"

"*Da Englisch* are those who are not Amish."

"I'm not English. I'm an Okie and proud of it."

"What is Okie?"

"Means I'm a cowboy from Oklahoma."

"Okie." Gideon grunted. "You are still *Englisch* to me."

Tully stood with the full pail of milk in his hand after finishing the last cow. "Now what?"

Gideon walked toward the back of the barn with two buckets in his hand. Tully followed him carrying the other two.

In the milk room, they poured the milk into a large strainer that emptied into one of the steel milk cans. They had enough milk to fill two of the large containers. Together they carried one of them out the door and placed it in the back of a cart, where there were already several more cans. Tully was surprised at how heavy they were.

Gideon was taken with another coughing fit. He had

to sit down on the back of the cart to catch his breath. Tully suspected something was seriously wrong. "Have you seen a doctor about that cough?"

"It's getting better."

Somehow Tully knew that wasn't the truth. He followed Gideon up to the house. The moment Tully opened the kitchen door, he was surrounded by delicious, mouthwatering aromas. Bacon frying, fresh baked bread and perking coffee. His stomach rumbled like an M2 Bradley fighting vehicle. Annabeth giggled, gave him a shy smile and retreated to stand beside her mother.

Gideon hung his hat and coat on one of several wooden pegs by the door. Tully did the same. Then Gideon showed Tully where to wash up. They might milk by hand, but the family had a modern bathroom with hot and cold running water. When he made his way back to the kitchen, he saw a refrigerator, but Becca was cooking on a wood-burning stove. He took a seat at the table and let his curiosity get the better of him.

"I've heard the Amish don't use electricity, so how is it that you have a fridge?"

"Our church allows members to use propane or natural gas for appliances."

"Then why are you cooking on a wood-burning stove?"

She carried a plate of bacon and sausage to the table. "Propane is expensive. Wood only costs our labor to cut and haul it. How do you like your eggs?"

"What are my choices?"

"Dippy, hard or scrambled."

He arched one eyebrow. "What is a dippy egg?"

"One that the yolk is runny enough to dip your bread

in. What do you call an egg cooked that way?" She tilted her head to the side. He found the gesture endearing.

"Over easy. The cook turns it over easy enough not to break the yolk."

"Isn't it funny that we have different names for the same things?"

"I never thought about it, but yes. I'll have my eggs scrambled, if it isn't too much trouble."

Annabeth sat down at the table across from him. "That's the way I cook mine."

He smiled at her. "Is that so?"

Gideon came in and took his place at the head of the table. He spoke to Annabeth in what sounded like German, but Tully recognized only about half the words. He was pretty sure *pride* was one of them. Annabeth looked chastised and remained silent.

When all the food was on the table, Becca sat at the foot of the table and bowed her head. Tully noticed they all did, but no one said grace out loud. He sat still, feeling ill at ease. Finally Gideon looked up and said, "Eggs."

Becca passed the plate to him. Annabeth helped herself to a generous portion and handed the rest to Tully. He took some but wanted to leave room for the toast and bacon. Once he started eating, he didn't want to stop. Everything tasted so much better than it had at the rehab facility or any army mess hall. The bacon was crisp. The eggs were fluffy. The toast was homemade bread the likes of which he hadn't tasted since his childhood, when his grandmother baked every Thursday. The strawberry jam was bursting with sweetness.

He caught Becca staring at him. He laid his fork down. "This is a mighty fine meal."

"I'm pleased that you like it," she said softly.

He tore his glance away from her pretty face flushed with the heat of the stove and looked at Annabeth. *"Wie geht es deinen eiern?"*

Annabeth's jaw dropped. "You speak *Deitsh*?"

"I speak a little. Did I get it right? What did I say?"

"You asked how are my…something. I didn't know the last word."

"I was trying to ask, how are your eggs?"

"Oiyah is eggs," Becca said.

"Oiyah, I'll have to remember that. I lived in Germany for two years. I knew a woman who taught the language to corporate big shots. She gave me lessons. I don't think it's the same German you people speak."

Gideon chuckled. "I've met a few tourists from Germany. I couldn't understand half of what they said, nor they me."

"I thought you folks spoke Pennsylvania Dutch."

"Deitsh isn't Dutch at all, but that's what folks call it," Becca said.

"We *Englisch*?" he asked.

She looked up and grinned. *"Ja,* you *Englisch.*"

"Nee, he is Okie," Gideon said.

Annabeth's eyes grew round. "What's that?"

"Das ist the proper name for a cowboy from Oklahoma," Gideon said solemnly, as if he had known all along what the term meant.

Tully couldn't look at Gideon for fear he would burst out laughing. There was a brief conversation in *Deitsh* between all of them. Becca and Annabeth nodded in understanding, but they didn't fill him in. It was definitely not the German language he had learned.

"Are you a real cowboy?" Annabeth asked with wonder in her wide eyes.

"Yes, ma'am. I grew up on a working ranch that my family homesteaded in 1893 called the Diamond X. Can't get much more cowboy than that."

When everyone was finished eating, Becca stood and began to clear the table. Tully jumped to his feet and began to help. From the expression on everyone's faces, he figured he'd done something else wrong. "It's okay if I help with the dishes, isn't it?"

Becca handed him her plate. "More than okay. Take note of how it's done, Gideon."

"I'll never hear the end of this. I'm going to take the milk to the co-op." He pushed back in his chair.

Becca grinned at his gruff retort and turned to Annabeth. "You may go along with Gideon."

Annabeth grinned. "Okay, but I have to go say goodbye to little Diamond first."

"That's her name, is it?" Becca asked with a sidelong glance at Tully.

"Is that okay?" Annabeth frowned slightly.

"Maybe it's a bit fancy."

"But she has a white diamond-shaped spot on her forehead," Annabeth said.

"Okay, Diamond it is. Hurry and get your coat. Don't keep Gideon waiting."

Becca moved to stand beside Tully at the sink. She dried the plate he handed her and gave him a questioning smile. "Is it permitted to name a calf after your family's ranch?"

She had a dimple in each cheek when she smiled. He wanted her to smile more often.

"It's perfectly acceptable to me," he said. "I'm honored."

"All right. *Danki*. I mean, thank you."

"I should get out of your hair." He handed her the last plate. "I'll be down at the barn if you need anything."

"You don't have to watch over her. We can do that."

"I feel responsible. I can't leave without knowing that she'll be okay…or not."

"If you feel strongly about it, I won't try to discourage you."

He slipped on his coat and settled his hat on his head. He touched the brim as he nodded to her. "Thanks again for breakfast, ma'am. You're a mighty fine cook." He went out the door without waiting for her reply.

After Gideon and Annabeth returned, Becca tried to act as if it were any other Sunday without a church service. She listened as Gideon read from the Bible, but her mind kept drifting. How long was Tully going to stay? Where would he go when he left? Her eyes were drawn to the kitchen window, but she didn't get up to see if he had gone.

Gideon closed the Bible. "Why don't you sing for us, Annabeth? Perhaps some of the songs you are learning for your Christmas program."

Annabeth happily sang several carols. When she was done, Becca joined her in singing some of their favorite hymns. It forced Becca to stay away from the kitchen window. When they finished an old German hymn, Annabeth looked up at her with bright eyes. "Maybe Tully would like to sing with us. I can go ask him."

Gideon shook his head. Annabeth's smile faded. When noon rolled around, Becca fixed a light lunch for the family. Although it was normal to spend the off Sunday afternoon visiting neighbors or friends, she hadn't made plans to go out and had quietly asked members of the community not to visit. Becca wanted Gideon to rest.

He finished his sandwich and took a sip of his coffee. "Is the *Englischer* still here?"

"I don't know," she was able to answer honestly. She was dying to find out. She hadn't heard his car start up, so she was reasonably certain he was still watching over the calf.

"Annabeth, look out the door and see if the outsider has gone," he said.

The child jumped up, raced to the door and pulled it open. "His car is still here, but I don't see him."

Gideon nodded slowly. "I reckon that means the calf hasn't improved. Becca, why don't you take him something to eat? I believe I will lie down for a bit."

Although she was tempted to jump up as eagerly as Annabeth had done, Becca calmly fixed another sandwich and poured some coffee in a thermos.

"Can I come with you?" Annabeth asked hopefully.

"Not this time. You can start on the dishes and then I will help you learn your lines for the Christmas play."

"Teacher says I have the most lines of anybody. I hope I can remember them all."

"You will if you practice enough." Becca put on her coat and scarf and went out.

The sunshine was bright off the snow-covered ground, but it gave little warmth. Winter in their new home had arrived in mid-November and now had a firm grip on the land. She hurried across the yard, pulled open the barn door and stepped into the dim interior.

It was noticeably warmer inside the snug barn thanks to the body heat of eleven large cows contently munching on their hay.

Becca heard Tully before she saw him. "Come on, sweet stuff, you can do it. Your mama has all the nice milk you could ever want. All you have to do is latch on and help yourself. That's it. Now you're getting the hang of it."

"How is she?" Becca opened the stall door and slipped inside. Tully was on the other side of Rosie, holding the baby upright with a sling made from a burlap sack.

"She has made a little progress but not enough. I was about to come up and ask for a bottle to feed her with."

"I'll get one for you. In the meantime I brought you some lunch." She held out the plate and thermos. "Church spread and coffee."

"That was thoughtful, but I'm not hungry. Not after that huge breakfast. The coffee sounds good, though." He looked up from the calf he was holding. "What is church spread?"

"A sandwich made with peanut butter, marshmallow crème and corn syrup. It's really good."

"Sounds good. Okay, Diamond, I'm gonna let you rest now." He carried her to the far corner of the stall and settled her in a mound of hay. She bawled pitifully. He sank down on the bedding beside her and stroked her head. "This nice lady is going to get you a bottle. You won't have to try to stand on that sore leg."

Rosie moved restlessly back and forth. Tully had made a halter from a length of rope and had her secured to the manger. Becca handed him the coffee and the plate. "I'll milk Rosie. We can give that to the calf. It's better for the little one than the milk replacer."

Becca went to the milk room. Inside she found the clean bottles and nipples in a cabinet by the sink. Taking a bucket and a milking stool, she carried her supplies to the stall, where Tully was sipping coffee from the thermos lid.

She saw he had taken a bite of the sandwich. "How is it?"

"The coffee is great. The church spread is a little too sweet for me. I imagine the kids love it."

She chuckled. "They do. So do most adults, myself included."

"Must be an acquired taste. Have you ever tried fry bread?"

She put the stool beside Rosie, sat down with her head pressed to the cow's warm flank and began milking. "I haven't. What is it?"

"It's a type of dough that's deep-fried. I love mine covered with powdered sugar or cinnamon and sugar. Sometimes I dip it in honey. It works to make tacos, too."

"We have tacos once in a while."

"You should try using fry bread instead of taco shells."

She looked his way. "You must send me the recipe."

"I'll do that."

She finished milking Rosie and poured some of the milk into the bottle. "Where are you going when you leave here?"

"I'm on my way to visit a friend in Caribou."

She handed him the bottle as she sank to her knees on the other side of the calf. "Will he or she be worried that you haven't arrived?"

Tully shook his head. "I wasn't sure how long it would take me to drive there from Philadelphia, so Arnie isn't expecting me just yet."

"Is Philadelphia your home?"

"It was temporarily. I'm sort of between residences right now." He gave the calf his attention as he tried to insert the nipple in her mouth. A lot leaked onto his hands before she figured out how it was supposed to work.

His face lit up with a bright smile of relief. "I think she's got it. Her chances of getting better just improved."

The words were barely out of his mouth before the calf let go of the nipple and began coughing. Her head sank to the hay. He rubbed the white patch on her forehead. "It's supposed to go suck, swallow, breathe. Don't be so greedy."

"How is she?" Annabeth asked from outside the stall.

Becca scowled at her. "I thought you were practicing for your school play."

"I got worried when you didn't come back in. You said you would help me."

Becca realized she had been gone much longer than she'd expected. "I guess I lost track of time."

She held out her hand, and Annabeth came into the stall. She sank to her knees beside Becca and stroked the calf's neck. "Is she getting better?"

"She's not feeling the best," Tully said. "I don't blame her. Having a broken leg can't be any fun."

"I had a splinter in my foot once. It wasn't any fun at all," Annabeth said solemnly.

Becca shared an amused glance with Tully. He managed to keep a straight face. "That must have been awful for you."

"*Mamm* got it out with her tweezers. *Daadi* said I hollered up a storm before it was over."

"I imagine I would holler, too," he said, letting a tiny smile slip out.

Annabeth didn't seem to notice as she continued to stroke the calf. "Is she going to get better?"

Becca slipped her arm around Annabeth's shoulders. "We will do what we can for Diamond. The rest is up to *Gott*."

"What if He's too busy looking after people to take care of a little calf?"

"*Gott* is never too busy. He cares for all creatures. We can't know His plan for Diamond or for any of us."

"Did He plan for her to get hurt?"

Becca had struggled with that same question when her husband died. How could such a thing be part of God's plan for her family? She hugged her daughter and closed her eyes to hold back the sting of tears. "He allowed it to happen. We must accept His will even if we don't understand why."

Annabeth sighed. "Okay. Are you coming in to help me practice my part for Christmas?"

Becca nodded. "You run along. I'll be in shortly."

Her child jumped up. "*Danki* for taking care of Diamond, Tully."

"I'm happy to do it," he said.

After Annabeth left Becca wiped her eyes, got to her feet and dusted the hay from her coat. "If you want to be on your way, Tully, we can look after her."

"I know that. I know it wasn't my fault she was in the road and that I hit her, but I feel guilty about it anyway. I don't mind staying. I've missed being around cattle. I didn't realize how much until now."

"In that case, you are welcome to stay as long as you like. Come up to the house when you get hungry."

"Can I ask you a personal question?"

She nodded. "I may not answer, but you can ask."

"What happened to your husband?"

She stared at him intently and saw only compassion in his eyes. She crossed her arms and stared at her feet. She didn't have to tell him anything, but she felt compelled to share her story. "My husband, his parents and his brother were coming home from visiting some neighbors when their buggy was struck by a speeding pickup that ran a stop sign. I saw it. My husband and his brother died instantly. My mother-in-law died a short time later. Gideon spent many days in the hospital."

She opened her eyes and saw a stricken expression cross his face before he looked away. "I'm sorry."

"*Gott* allowed it. I have accepted it."

"What happened to the driver of the pickup?"

"He didn't have a scratch on him," she said, letting an edge of bitterness out with her words and regretting it instantly. "I have forgiven him."

Her throat closed with grief. She hurried out of the stall before Tully could see her tears.

Chapter Four

Tully cringed as Becca hurried away from him. He pulled his jacket tighter across his chest. He couldn't keep his curiosity about her in check, and he'd upset her again. He rubbed Diamond's soft ear. "You need to get better so I can leave these good people in peace."

The afternoon stretched into the evening. Gideon and Becca came in to do the second round of milking for the day, but they didn't linger. He was able to feed Diamond a little more the next time she showed signs of interest in the bottle. When it grew dark, he started wishing for a heavier coat and a flashlight. He hadn't exactly thought this plan through. He had his arms crossed and was stomping his booted feet when Becca came in carrying a kerosene lantern and a heavy quilt.

She hung the light from a nail high on the wall, bathing the area in a soft golden glow. "I thought the baby might be getting cold."

"I don't know about her, but I am."

"Then this will help, unless you have regained your senses and intend to come into the house with us."

Becca's bundle was actually two quilts. She handed one to Tully.

"Can I bring the calf in with me?" Tully wrapped the blue-and-white quilt around his shoulders while Becca spread the other one over Diamond.

"I do not approve of having a cow in my kitchen, even a little cow."

He nodded. "That's what I figured."

"Her ears are up. Her eyes look brighter." She stroked the calf's neck.

"I gave her another dose of pain medication about half an hour ago. It seems to be helping. She took a little more from the bottle this time. Now if she would only stand and nurse on her mother, my job would be done."

"You have done more than enough. Go up to the house and get warm. I will be her *kinder heeda* for a while."

"*Kinder* means 'children,' but I don't know *heeda*."

She smiled. "The one who watches the children when the parents are gone."

"Babysitter?"

"*Ja*, I will be the babysitter." She sat on the milking stool she'd left earlier. "You can take the lamp with you. I don't mind the dark."

The calf put her head down and closed her eyes. Seeing Becca prepared to stay made him realize he was being foolish. The calf had eaten and was going to sleep for a few hours. He wasn't needed and neither was Becca. He could sit in a warm kitchen and come out to check on her every hour or so.

"I think she'll be fine on her own for a while. You don't need to stay with her."

Becca looked surprised. "You'll come in for a while?"

"I will." Tully hugged his quilt around his shoulders as he followed Becca out of the barn into the clear, cold night. The rising quarter moon illuminated the buildings, snow-covered fields, woods and pasture in stark black and white. He took in the beauty of the night, and something clicked inside him. God had created a stunningly beautiful world that Tully Lange had failed to appreciate for far too long.

He drew a deep breath of the clean air and slowly blew it out as a white mist that rose over his head. Maybe God's plan for little Diamond was simply to make one jaded cowboy stop long enough to appreciate the beauty of the world around him.

Becca looked back at him. "Is something wrong?"

"I was noticing how pretty the night is." And how lovely she was with her face bathed in the lantern light.

"It's a nice view, but the cold takes getting used to. It's much different from our last home."

"Where was that?"

"Pinecrest, Florida."

"Florida?" He burst out laughing. "You moved to Maine from Florida? Not just Maine but northern Maine?"

She giggled. "Sounds silly when you put it that way, but I have lived in many states. Ohio, Pennsylvania, Maryland. My husband had a restless streak."

"So why Maine?"

"My grandfather, Samuel Yoder, is one of the founders of this new Amish community. He wrote to us when he saw this dairy farm was for sale. The price was reasonable. Gideon had owned his own dairy before the accident. We sold what we didn't need and came here. This is where I intend to stay. This is where I want Annabeth to grow up. We don't get the tourists like the Amish settlements in Ohio and Pennsylvania do. Here we don't have to put up with outsiders gawking at us."

Her eyes widened, and she clapped her gloved hand over her mouth. "I didn't mean that the way it sounded."

"As an outsider, I take no offense. I'll try to keep my curiosity in check."

"I don't mind your curiosity." She started walking toward the house again.

"You don't? I thought I upset you earlier."

She stopped again to face him. "Grief is like that. Sometimes the least little thing will catch me off guard and remind me of the man I loved and lost. I was not upset with you."

"But my question brought it to mind."

"He is never far from my thoughts. If not you, then Annabeth or Gideon will do or say something that reminds me of him every day. Time heals the hurt, but it cannot make me forget. Come. It is too cold to have this discussion out here."

He marveled at her calm strength and acceptance as he followed her to the house. Inside he found the kitchen almost stifling after the chill of being outside. He laid his quilt aside and took off his fleece-lined jean jacket. He hung it next to his hat on the pegs by the door.

She was at the stove stirring something that smelled delicious. "I saved some chicken and rice for you. Sit."

"Yes, ma'am." He pulled out a chair and sat down as he yawned widely. The heat was making him sleepy. He'd driven all night the previous day, and he hadn't had so much as a nap today.

He blinked hard and found her staring at him. "You're tired."

"A mite. Where is everyone?"

"Gone to bed." She put a steaming bowl of chicken, rice and chopped vegetable in front of him. "Eat and then stretch out on the sofa. I will wake you in an hour."

He realized he was too tired to argue with her. He nodded mutely and dug into the food. A glass of milk appeared beside his plate. He looked up and caught her smiling at him. "I like to see someone enjoying my cooking."

He raised his spoon. "This is better than my grandma used to make. I didn't think that was possible."

"Danki."

He gazed into her pretty green eyes. "I'm the one that should be thanking you."

Becca looked away first. "It's only a little warmed-over chicken and rice."

"Your kindness is about the only thing that tops your cooking."

She knew she must be blushing. She turned away and busied herself at the sink. "Enough talk. Finish eating and get some sleep."

"Only if you promise not to let me sleep too long. I'm afraid Diamond will start missing me. I've been telling her cowpoke jokes all afternoon. Did you know in Oklahoma we use a crowbar to tell how hard the wind is blowing?"

"What?"

"Yes, ma'am. We got a hole in the side of the house. If we want to know how windy it is, we stick the crowbar out."

"And what does that tell you?"

"If the crowbar is bent when we pull it in, the wind is

about normal. If it's broke, it's best not to go out, 'cause our hats will end up in another state. I have at least six in Texas, I reckon."

Becca smiled. "Eat. Be funny later."

"Yes, ma'am."

He was quiet for a little while, but then she heard him push back from the table. "Thanks again for the grub."

After he went into the other room, she sat down at the table and opened her prayer book. After reading for a half hour, she got up to check on Tully. He was curled on his side on the sofa with her quilt snuggled underneath his chin. He reminded her of a little boy. She listened to his even breathing and then went upstairs to her bedroom. She laid down without undressing, knowing she wasn't going to get much sleep. She dozed off for a while and then jerked awake. The battery-operated clock on her bedside table showed it was just after midnight.

She crept downstairs and saw Tully hadn't needed her to wake him. He was already gone. She was tempted to go out to the barn just to visit with him again but realized she was being foolish. She went back upstairs and slept soundly until five thirty, her usual time for rising.

She put on the coffee and brought in the milk pails to scrub them with soapy water and bleach. She was just finishing up when Gideon came in.

"*Guder mariye*, Becca. Has our friend gone?"

"Good morning, Gideon. I looked out a little while ago, and his car was still here."

He got into his heavy coat and took several pails from her. "I reckon I'll see how his little patient is doing. The man sure has his heart set on seeing her get better."

"As does Annabeth." Becca put on her scarf and

heavy coat, picked up the rest of the pails, and followed him out to start the morning milking.

They met Tully coming in. He looked tired. "How is she?" Becca asked.

He smiled, and she realized how handsome he was with a grin on his face. "Standing on her own, nursing like a champ. It looks like she's gonna be just fine."

Gideon patted Tully's shoulder. "That's *wunderbar.*"

"She came out of her slump about two in the morning. She hasn't slowed down since. She's even making a few attempts to run. Now I will say goodbye and get on the road."

She heard the reluctance to say that farewell in his voice—or maybe she only wanted to hear it. "You will not go anywhere until you've had your breakfast. No arguing. The coffee is ready. We will be back when the milking is done."

She couldn't be sure, but she thought he looked relieved. He tipped his hat to her. "You'll get no argument from me on that score. I have already tasted your cooking."

Becca rushed through the morning milking, getting a few protests from the cows for her hurried actions. She set the final bucket down in the milk room for Gideon to strain. "I'm going to go start breakfast."

Up at the house, she found Tully and Annabeth at the table. Annabeth was laughing. "You tell good stories, Tully. Tell me another one about your pony."

He leaned toward her. "My pony was so mean that I couldn't ride him barefoot because he would swing his head around and bite my toes to make me get off. If that didn't work, he would run under the clothesline and I would find myself sitting on the ground with Grandma's clean sheets over my head."

Annabeth grinned. "But your grandma wouldn't be mad at you, would she?"

"No, but she had a powerful lot of choice words for grandpa about his knowledge of horseflesh."

The child giggled. "My friend Maddie has a pony."

"I hope it's not a mean pony."

"Oh *nee*, she's a wonderful pony. *Daadi* says I can get a pony when I'm older so I can ride to school and *Mamm* won't have to drive me every day. Did you ride your pony to school?"

"Nope. The school bus came to pick me and my cousins up every day. It sure would've been more fun to ride the horse, but it was twenty-five miles to school."

Gideon came in and washed up. She heard him wheezing, and she glanced at him frequently. He turned to her as he dried his hands. "I'm getting old," he said in *Deitsh*. "I will let you help me load the milk cans." He spoke again in *Deitsh*, so she knew he didn't want Tully to understand.

"Of course." She watched him with concern but didn't want to say anything in front of Annabeth or Tully. After a few minutes, he seemed to recover and smiled at her. She dished up oatmeal loaded with raisins and pecans and put out the brown sugar for her daughter's sweet tooth. Tully didn't seem to have the same affliction, for he added only a sprinkling to his cereal.

The breakfast that morning was one of the most pleasant times she had enjoyed in her new home. Meals were normally a quiet time, but Tully had them all laughing with his tall tales of growing up in what he called the Wildest West. Becca wasn't sure how much was real and how much was embellished to make the story better. She was sorry when everyone finished eating.

She carried the dishes to the sink. "Annabeth, get ready for school."

"Okay." She headed to her room.

Gideon finished his coffee. "I'd better get the milk loaded."

"If you wait a minute, I'll help," she offered.

"*Nee*, I'm fine now. Tully, you have been an interesting guest. Come back and visit us someday soon." Gideon held out his hand.

Tully stood and shook it. "I'll do that."

After Gideon went out, Becca stacked the dishes in the sink and then laid her towel aside. She couldn't put off the moment any longer. "I'd better get the horse hitched or Annabeth will be late to school. I have enjoyed meeting you, Tully Lange. I will think of you kindly each time I see Rosie's new calf."

"I'll think fondly of you and your family." He looked around the kitchen. "It's been a long time since I've been in a place that feels like a real home."

Pity stirred in her chest at the sorrow in his voice. "What kind of places have you lived in if they haven't been homes?"

"Army bases—army housing, mostly. Apartments. Some good, some not so good."

"You were a soldier?" She recoiled in shock. Such a profession went against everything her religion stood for.

"You say that like it's a bad word."

She dropped her gaze, ashamed of her unkind reaction. "I didn't mean to criticize. We Amish believe in peace, in turning the other cheek. We are conscientious objectors to any kind of war."

"I see. Then I'm glad I didn't tell you until now."

She caught his arm before he turned away, stunned at her boldness, but she needed to make him understand. "If you had told me the minute we met, you would not have been treated differently by me or any Amish person."

"Sure. That's why your jaw dropped."

"I will admit you took me by surprise. I had a moment when I couldn't reconcile your tenderness for an injured baby calf to someone who could take a human life in war."

"And now you can?"

"Now I see the man in front of me. I see Tully Lange, a kind and helpful person. I cannot judge you, for only God knows what is in any man's heart."

"Thanks." He gazed into her eyes with such gentle longing…almost sadness.

What did he see? What was it that he wanted? He was about to walk out of her life forever. Would he find a place he could call home, or would he be like her departed husband, unable to settle anywhere? It saddened her that she would never know if he found peace.

She resisted the urge to lay her hand on his cheek and comfort him. Why was she drawn to this stranger?

He turned away and slipped into his coat, then took his hat from the peg by the door. He settled it on his head. When he looked at her from beneath the brim, his eyes were no longer sad. They held a glint of humor. "Becca Beachy, your cooking was worth all the trouble your cows gave me."

He opened the door and stepped outside. A second

later he turned to her. "Something has happened to Gideon." He took off down the steps at a run.

Becca looked out the door and saw Gideon lying on the ground beside the milk cart. She ran after Tully and was relieved to see Gideon trying to get up. He gripped his leg with both hands as he grimaced in pain.

She stepped around the spilled milk can. "What happened?"

Tully supported Gideon with an arm around his waist. "Did you hurt yourself?"

"My bad leg gave out on me. I tried to keep the milk from falling, but the can twisted, and that's when I fell."

"Is it broken?" Becca asked, feeling it gently.

"It hurts in my knee. I can't move my leg."

Tully looked at Becca. "Get Annabeth and get in my car. His knee is dislocated. He needs a doctor."

"I don't," Gideon protested.

Tully placed Gideon's arm around his shoulder. "I've seen this kind of thing before, and you do. Stubbornness is a form of pride, old man. Get in the car."

Becca was relieved to let Tully take over. If it had been only her, Gideon would not have sought treatment. She opened the front door of the house and called for Annabeth. Her daughter came running. "What's the matter, *Mamm*? You sound scared."

"Your grandfather has been hurt. Tully is taking us to the doctor."

She hurried Annabeth outside, and they got into the back seat of Tully's car.

He turned in the seat to look at her. "Where is the nearest ER?"

"Presque Isle. Head toward New Covenant, the same

way the cows went, only go straight at the crossroads where they turned."

They reached the city thirty minutes later, and Becca directed him to the emergency center. He helped Gideon hobble inside.

They were fortunate that the emergency room wasn't busy. A doctor was able to examine Gideon within fifteen minutes. After X-rays, the doctor finally came in to speak to them twenty minutes later.

"Your knee is dislocated. Some of your ligaments are torn. I can relocate the joint, but it isn't going to be pleasant. After that I'm going to put you in a brace that you'll need to wear for the next four weeks. Use ice to keep the swelling down. The cough is also a serious matter. You have pneumonia. I'm surprised you are out of bed. I'd like to put you in the hospital for some antibiotics, but I suspect you'll refuse."

"I will. I have a dairy herd to take care of," Gideon said firmly.

"Find someone else to do that. No heavy lifting. I don't want you picking up anything heavier than a five-pound sack of flour until Christmas." He wrote on a pad and handed Becca two prescriptions. "This is for the antibiotic. See that he takes them four times a day, and this one will help the pain. Someone will be in to fit him for a pair of crutches."

She nodded mutely. She didn't have the money to pay for the ER visit, let alone pain pills. They moved Gideon into a wheelchair. At the billing office, Becca explained that she would have to have their bishop raise the money to pay the bill.

The kindly woman behind the desk smiled. "We've learned the Amish pay their bills. Don't worry. I've dealt with Bishop Schultz before. I'll send him a letter by the end of the week. Take your prescriptions to the hospital pharmacy. They will fill them and add them to your bill. I'll let them know you are coming."

Becca nodded and turned back to Tully. "Can you take us home after that?"

His eyes were troubled. "Of course. Anything you need. You don't have insurance?"

She shook her head. "*Nee*, we do not."

"Let me guess. It's not your way."

"We take care of each other. Our congregation will hold a collection for us." She didn't expect him to understand. Part of her wanted to lean on him for the support he offered, but the other part knew she needed to avoid becoming more involved with him. He was an outsider.

"What about the dairy?" he asked.

"Our neighbors will help. We will manage." She hoped her tone closed the subject. She might insist they would be fine, but she knew it would be a struggle to get the work done and keep Gideon from trying to do too much. The Lord was testing her once again. This time she would be stronger, but was she strong enough?

Tully kept glancing at Becca's face in his rearview mirror as he drove them home. She looked like she had the weight of the world on her shoulders. It must seem that way to her. Would the community help as much as she predicted? What if they didn't? He could see her trying to do it all by herself.

It wasn't like it was his concern. She wasn't part of his family or even a military spouse. He had done all he could to help by saving her calf and gathering her strayed cattle. Arnie was expecting him. Not any certain day, but soon. He needed to see the one buddy who'd showed he still cared. Arnie's occasional card or phone call had meant the world when there was no one else.

He turned in to the Beachy farm and pulled up in front of the house. Becca and Annabeth helped Gideon out of the car. Becca waved Tully away. "We have delayed you long enough. Do not worry about us. We are in God's hands. Our faith is in His mercy."

"Okay. Annabeth, I may stop in some day and see how Diamond is getting along. Take good care of her for me."

"I will."

Gideon moved slowly on his crutches with Becca and Annabeth hovering close beside him. They all went into the house.

Tully turned his car around and drove down the lane. He stopped and waited as two logging trucks blew past. Once the coast was clear, he still didn't move. He slipped the gearshift into Park. He looked into his rear-view mirror and saw Becca walking to the barn. She came out a few minutes later leading a horse. She had milk to take to the co-op and a child to take to school. The young widow had had her hands full even before Gideon fell.

She wasn't his problem. She didn't want his help. He had more than enough trouble without borrowing some from an Amish family. He was broke, out of work and homeless again. He had a friend, maybe his only friend, waiting to see him. Becca and her family would be taken care of by the other Amish. She had made that plain. She didn't need him.

No one had ever really needed him.

He put his car in gear.

Chapter Five

Tully stepped on the brake. He couldn't do it. He couldn't just drive away. She was going to get his help if she wanted it or not. He had made a lot of bad decisions in his life, but this wasn't going to be one of them. This time he was making the right choice. Maybe it was because she had suffered so much at the hands of a reckless driver and he was somehow trying to make amends for that. It wasn't rational, but it was what he needed to do. He shoved the car in Park. Picking up his phone, he dialed Arnie's number.

His buddy answered on the second ring. "Are you in town already, or have you chickened out? Wait. Who is this?"

Tully knew the drill. "This is Tully Lange. I'm an alcoholic. I've been sober for four months and one week."

"It still gives me chills to hear you say that. I'm proud of you, Cowboy."

"Thanks, man. That means a lot."

"So where are you?"

"I had to take a small detour."

"Oh yeah?"

"It wasn't a moose. It was a cow."

"You hit a cow?" Arnie didn't even try to control his laughter. "'Cowboy Cow Collision in Northern Maine.' It could make the national news."

"I didn't hit the cow, but I hit her calf and broke the little thing's leg. I took her to the closest farm. Turned out to be a dairy run by an Amish family. It was their cow. Look, the family is in a bind right now. The old man that runs the place got hurt. He has only his widowed daughter-in-law and his granddaughter to help him. I'm going to stick around for a while and give them a hand."

"Ah, there is a woman involved, isn't there?"

"Nothing like that."

"Sure. Is she pretty? Is it the widow or the granddaughter?"

"The granddaughter is in the first grade."

"So it's the widow. Tully, you sly dog."

Tully grew annoyed. "I said it's not like that."

"Okay, my bad. Stay and help the family for as long as they need it. You aren't likely to find a drink on an Amish farm."

It was a good point. "Look, I'll see you at Christmas. I just need to make sure they're going to be okay."

"Don't forget me, Cowboy."

Tully caught a note of sadness in his friend's voice. "You know I can't forget you. You saved my life."

"Twice," Arnie added emphatically.

"And you'll never let me forget it."

"That's right. You owe me big-time. Someday I'm gonna call in that marker."

Tully chuckled. "Any time you need someone to save your life, I'm your guy. See you in a few days."

He might have made a joke out of it, but Tully was serious. He owed Arnie more than he could ever repay. After ending his call, Tully turned the car around and drove into the Beachy farmyard again. He saw Becca and Annabeth lifting the heavy milk cans onto the back of a wagon. He got out of his car and lifted the last two steel containers onto the wagon bed for them.

Becca brushed the snow from her gloves and frowned at him. "I could have managed those. I thought you were leaving?"

"Ma'am, if you know anything about cowboys, you should know that we have a powerful sense of right and wrong. It is just plain wrong to leave a woman in a lurch if a fellow can help."

"I thank you for your offer, but don't concern yourself with us. Annabeth, get up on the seat. We need to get going." Becca moved to the front of the wagon. She ignored the hand Tully held out to help her up.

He looked at Annabeth and rolled his eyes. "Your mama is a stubborn one."

"Sometimes." The child held out her arms. Tully lifted her up beside her mother.

He pushed his hat up with one finger. "I've decided to stick around for a while. No point in telling me to move along, because I'm not going to do it. I'll be here when you get back. If you have any chores that need doing, tell me now."

She stared straight ahead. "None that I can think of."

He held back a smile. "Annabeth, can you think of any?"

"*Daadi* was going to split some kindling for the stove this morning."

Becca scowled at her daughter. "That's enough. It

was kind of you to offer, but your help isn't needed." She lifted the reins, spoke to the horse and headed the wagon down the lane.

Tully watched them until they reached the highway. Annabeth looked back and waved. Becca did not. Her rejection hurt more than it should.

"I like the cowboy," Annabeth said. "I'm glad he's going to stay. Aren't you? He can help with lots of chores so *Daadi* can rest."

Becca glanced at her daughter's face. "He won't be staying. We will do our own chores and Gideon's, too. We will just have to work harder until Gideon is better."

It was going to be difficult, but Becca had never shied away from hard work. Tully's offer to stay and help was kind, but she couldn't afford to pay a hired hand even for a week, let alone for the month that the doctor had said Gideon needed to heal.

Annabeth tipped her head to gaze at Becca. "Don't you like Tully?"

She liked him a lot. That was the trouble, but she couldn't tell her child that. She barely knew the man. "He has shown us great kindness. For that I'm grateful, but don't expect him to be at the farm when you get home from school."

Among the Amish such acts of charity were common. She wasn't used to seeing the same behavior from the *Englisch*. She didn't know what to make of him.

"I hope he will be there," Annabeth said wistfully. "He makes me laugh."

When they arrived at the school, the children were outside for the morning recess. Their teacher, Eva Coblentz, waved from the schoolhouse steps. Her brother

Danny stood beside her. Eva planned to marry after Christmas. Her brother would take over her teaching job when she left. Danny was single and a nice fellow. He had asked Becca to walk out with him several times. She had politely refused. She wasn't interested in stepping out with him or anyone. She had no intention of marrying again. Loving someone else didn't seem possible.

Danny gave Becca a warm smile as he walked over. "We were wondering what had become of Annabeth this morning. I was just about to drive out and check on you and your family."

Becca tipped her head slightly and avoided meeting his gaze, not wanting to give him any encouragement. "I appreciate your concern."

"Rosie had her calf, but Tully hit her baby with his car and broke her leg. Then *Daadi* Gideon slipped in the snow and hurt his knee and the cowboy took us to the hospital," Annabeth said all in a rush.

Danny's eyes widened. "It sounds like you've had a busy morning. How serious is Gideon's injury?"

Becca sighed. Danny would find out soon enough. "He dislocated his knee."

"That's not *goot*," Danny said. "Is there anything I can do?"

"*Nee*, we are fine."

He shook his head. "Nonsense. My cousin dislocated his knee two years ago. He was laid up for weeks, and he is a lot younger than Gideon. I'll come out to help with the chores before and after school."

"That's not necessary." This was exactly what she had hoped to avoid. Becca didn't want to spend her mornings and afternoons working alongside Danny.

Nor did she wish to spend weeks resisting his persistent attempts to get her to go out with him. He was a fine man, but she wasn't interested in him romantically.

He leaned closer. "Don't be prideful, Becca. Let me help." He held out his arms to Annabeth, who went to him happily.

Becca looked away. "It isn't pride. We…we already have a man helping us. An *Englisch* fellow."

Danny lowered Annabeth to the ground. She gaped at Becca. "The cowboy is staying? Before you said—"

Becca cut her short. "Never mind what I said."

A faint frown appeared on Danny's face. "Is it someone I know?"

"*Nee.* He is new to this area. Would you ask Bishop Schultz to come out to the dairy when you see him? I need to get this milk to the collection station, or I would go see him myself."

"I'll take care of it," Danny said. "And I will bring Annabeth home this afternoon so you don't have to make the trip."

She couldn't see a way to refuse his kind offer. *"Danki."*

Annabeth waved to her friend Maddie on the swings. "Guess what? I have a new calf. Her name is Diamond, and we have a real cowboy staying with us."

Becca knew the whole community would be curious about their visitor once the children took home Annabeth's information. She was sure to have visitors as soon as word got out about Gideon's injury. She would need to have a suitable story ready to explain Tully's presence. If he hadn't already left.

She thanked Danny and turned her horse around. The collection station was at the farm of an *Englisch* dairyman named LeBlanc some two miles past her own farm. He maintained refrigerated storage tanks that she and several other small dairies rented from him. The milk truck came three times a week to take the collected milk into the city to the processing plant. Thankfully he was in the building when she arrived. He emptied the milk cans for her.

Heading back to the farm, Becca kept her horse at a steady trot. A flutter of anticipation settled in her midsection as she turned into her lane. Would Tully be there?

As she drove into the farmyard, she saw his car was missing. She tried to ignore the letdown that seemed to sap her strength. She hadn't really expected him to stay. She wasn't sure why she was so disappointed.

She climbed down from the wagon stiffly. The cold seemed sharper than before. The sun slipped behind the clouds, making the morning gloomy. She unhitched the horse, checked on little Diamond, who seemed to be doing well with her cast, and then went into the house. She stopped on the threshold. Tully was down on one knee filling the kindling box beside her stove.

He rose to his feet and dusted off his gloves. "If that's not enough, I'll bring in another armload."

He was still here. "I thought you had gone. Your car isn't here."

"Gideon told me to put it in the shed because it is going to snow. He's doing okay. I had him take two of those pain pills, although he wasn't happy about it. I put an ice pack on his leg. He's a hard man to keep down." He shifted nervously from foot to foot. "I threatened to hog-tie him if he got up without help again. Is this enough wood?"

"That is fine for now. Tully, I appreciate all you have done."

"It's nothing."

She moved to take off her coat and thick woolen scarf and hung them up. "It is much more than nothing. Please sit down." She gestured toward the table.

He took a seat and waited for her to speak. She sat across from him with her hands folded on the table in front of her. She didn't like discussing their financial situation, but she didn't feel she had a choice. "I would like you to stay until Gideon is better, but you must understand that we cannot afford to pay you for your help."

He leaned back in his chair. A wry smile curved his lips and showed a dimple in his right cheek. "A few days of your good cooking will be payment enough. You don't have to worry about putting me up. I can sleep in the barn if the animals don't mind my snoring."

"Why are you doing this?"

His smile disappeared. His eyes grew serious. He leaned forward and clasped his hands together on the tabletop. "I wasn't exaggerating when I said it had been a long time since I was somewhere that felt like a home. When I got out of the army two years ago, things didn't go well for me. Let's just say I messed up. I ended up homeless and living out of my car. I know what it feels like to be down and out. You folks have hit a rough patch. Somebody gave me a helping hand when I needed it. I'd like to think I'm repaying that favor by helping you and your family. Just until Gideon is back on his feet. I'm serious about sleeping in the barn. I've slept in worse places."

What places and why? She longed to ask him, but she didn't. It was unlikely that she would ever know the answers, but the pain he tried to hide underneath his words touched her deeply. "That won't be necessary. We have a spare bedroom you can use, but I must talk this over with Gideon before I can give you an answer."

"Fair enough." It wasn't an outright no. Tully relaxed a fraction. He was prepared to leave if she insisted. He didn't want to stay if he made her uncomfortable.

"What do you need to discuss with me?" Gideon asked as he slowly made his way into the kitchen on his crutches.

Tully scowled at him. "What did I say would happen if you got up without help?"

"Tying the hog is not needed." Gideon lowered himself slowly onto a chair. "As you can see, I have managed on my own. What are the two of you talking about?"

Tully glanced at Becca. When she didn't explain, he did. "We were discussing my staying on to help with chores for a few days until you get back on your feet."

"I am on my feet."

Tully scoffed. "You're barely on one foot and two crutches. Explain to me how you are going to feed and milk your cows."

"He has a point," Becca said. "If he wants to help us, we should let him."

"We can't pay him. A laborer is worthy of his hire."

"Room and board will be sufficient payment for me. I don't know much about dairy cattle. I may end up being more trouble than I'm worth."

A smile tugged at the corner of Becca's mouth. "If that becomes the case, I will stop feeding you."

He grinned at her. "And I will be gone before nightfall. Now that you know how to get rid of me, what chores need to be done?"

"I will show you." Gideon attempted to rise, but he grimaced and sank back onto his chair. "Perhaps Becca should show you what you need to do."

"I will after we get you back into bed," Becca said, motioning for Tully to help her. Between the two of them, they were able to get Gideon up on his crutches and into his bedroom. Tully stood back and waited as she carefully propped Gideon's injured leg on a pair of pillows and pulled a quilt over him.

She stood beside the bed looking uncertain. "Is there anything you need? Do you want another pain pill?"

"I'm fine for now. Don't fuss over me."

She tucked the quilt around his shoulders. "I will fuss over whomever I please. Promise me you won't try to get up until we are back in the house."

"I promise. Now go away and let me sleep." He closed his eyes and turned his face away from them.

Tully stepped out into the hall. Becca followed him and closed the door. A second later she opened it a crack. "I want to be able to hear him if he calls out."

Tully longed to offer her some measure of comfort or reassurance, but he wasn't sure what to say. Comfort hadn't been a big part of his life. His grandfather had been fond of saying, "Be tough, boy, because life is tougher." The army hadn't been big on coddling, either. He cleared his throat and took a stab at it. "He's a strong man. He'll get over this."

"I pray you are right." She turned away from the door.

"What made you decide to let me stay?"

She wouldn't look at him. "Annabeth wants to hear more stories about your cowboy ways."

He sensed it wasn't the whole truth. "That's nice to hear, but I don't believe it's why you changed your mind."

"I have my reasons." She propped her fists on her hips. "Do you want to stay or don't you?"

He held both hands up. "I want to stay, but only if I won't make more trouble for you."

She rolled her eyes and shook her head. "All men do is make more trouble."

He had to laugh. It was the wrong thing to do.

She scowled at him and pointed to the end of the hall. "Your room is there. I have baking and laundry to do. Stay out of the kitchen."

She spun on her heels and walked away.

"You had better do as she says," Tully heard Gideon say.

He pushed open the door to make sure Gideon wasn't trying to get up again. "I know how to follow orders."

"That is *goot*. When Becca is in a mood, you had best avoid her. If you can't, do what she says. My wife was the same way. I blamed it on her red hair."

Tully stared toward the kitchen, where he could hear pots and pans being rattled about. "I seem to have a knack for upsetting Becca."

Gideon chuckled. "Don't feel bad. My son used to say the same thing."

Tully moved to stand beside the bed. He pushed his hands into the front pockets of his jeans. "Becca told me what happened to your family. I'm real sorry."

"They are with *Gott*. As we all shall be when He wills it." Gideon raised himself up in bed and scooted back to lean against the headboard. "Why didn't you go on your way?"

Tully couldn't admit the whole truth. "I like you folks. I couldn't leave without trying to help."

"Our community will take care of us." Gideon made a sour face.

"You don't sound thrilled about that."

"Charity is much harder to accept than to give. I sometimes suffer from the sin of pride." Gideon gestured to his leg up on pillows. "When I prayed *Gott* would help me overcome it, I wasn't expecting this to be His answer."

"I know what you mean. I don't want to add to Becca's workload. I hope you'll steer me in the right direction."

"Can you cook, clean, darn socks and do laundry?"

"I can do all that. My grandma made me learn to take care of myself on the ranch, but I'm a lousy cook."

Gideon chuckled. "When I see something that needs to be done, I will tell you. When Becca sees something that needs to be done, she does it herself. You will help best by getting out of her way."

"Got it. Thanks for the advice. What can I do for you?"

"How good are you at checkers?"

"Pretty good, if I do say so myself."

"There is a board and pieces in the desk in the living room. Bring it in here. We shall see if the Lord will help you overcome your sin of pride."

"If that's a convoluted way of saying you think you can beat me, I'll show you a thing or two."

Becca came to the door. "Gideon, you are supposed

to be resting. I'm going to take the trash out to the burn barrel."

"I'll do that," Tully said quickly.

She glanced at each of them and then went away.

Tully looked at Gideon. "Where is the burn barrel?"

"Behind the shed where I had you put your car."

"I'll be back with the checkers set in a bit." Tully went down the hall to the kitchen. Becca was at the table cracking an egg into a mixing bowl. She glanced up at him and tossed the shell into the overflowing trash can. It rolled out and hit the floor.

Tully jumped to pick it up as Becca bent to do the same. His hand closed over hers. He met her eyes, and they both straightened slowly. He still held her hand.

His heart started thudding heavily in his chest. His gaze swept over her face. What would it be like to kiss her?

Chapter Six

Becca's breath caught in her throat. She wanted to pull her hand away from Tully's grasp, but she didn't. She waited—for what, she wasn't sure. His eyes darkened and then softened as he gazed at her. She couldn't look away. She licked her dry lips and then pressed them tightly together. She wasn't a giddy teenage girl, but for a few seconds she felt like one again. Tully had put her completely off balance with the simple touch of his hand. Her head was reeling.

It wasn't supposed to be this way. He was an outsider. She barely knew him. Yet there was a connection between them that she couldn't explain. She was sure he felt it, too.

A shadow passed over his eyes. Regret? He looked away and took a step back. "Sorry."

So was she. Had their fragile friendship been damaged?

He pulled out the brown paper bag she used to line the trash can. "Shall I burn it, too?"

She dropped the eggshell on top of what he carried.

"*Nee*, but make sure the lid is on tight so animals don't get into it."

"Okay." He didn't look at her as he gathered his jacket off the peg and went outside.

Becca sat down and drew a shaky breath. What had just happened? She replayed the charged moment in her head. Had it been real?

He wasn't Amish. There couldn't be anything between them other than friendship or business dealings. Any other relationship was forbidden.

Should she insist that he leave? How would she explain her sudden change of mind to Tully? To Gideon?

He accidentally touched my hand and my knees went weak?

Gideon would think she had lost her mind.

She gripped her hands tightly together. Maybe that was the answer. Perhaps the stress of managing the dairy, Gideon's failing health and his injury—not to mention the bills that were piling up—had all come together and rattled her enough that she mistook a simple bit of light-headedness for a romantic reaction to Tully's touch.

She took several deep breaths and started to relax. Nothing had happened that couldn't be explained. She was being silly to imagine a mountain when there wasn't even a molehill. She had been pushing herself too hard. Gideon was always telling her that. Maybe it was time she listened.

She looked at the pans she had lined up to make coffee cakes for the people she knew would come to visit. She didn't need five cakes. Two would do. That would give her more time to get started on the laundry.

The outside door opened, and she jumped. Tully

looked in, and her heart started pounding. What did he think had passed between them? What should she say about it?

"The vet is here to look at the calf again. Do you want to hear what he has to say?"

"Of course." She was responsible for every aspect of the farm with Gideon confined to bed. She opened her mouth to tell him that and shut it again. She forced herself to let Tully handle this.

"On second thought, you can deal with him. Tell me later unless he needs to speak to me. I must get these cakes made before the bishop shows up. I'm sure he won't come alone."

"Sure. Happy to do that." He looked relieved and went out again.

"That wasn't so hard," she said aloud. Only it was. She cracked another egg into her bowl and resisted the urge to grab her coat and follow Tully outside. If he took her hand again, she would know for certain if her feelings were real or imagined. She closed her hands into fists and pushed them into her apron pockets. It would be better if a second touch never happened.

She was putting the filled pans in the oven when Tully came back in. "The vet just left."

"I hope he gave you good news."

"He did."

"Fine. I was about to go check on Gideon."

Tully took his coat off and hung up his hat. "I can do that. He wanted a game of checkers, unless you have something else I need to do."

"I can't think of anything." She found herself staring at the back of his head. He was avoiding her gaze. Was he uncomfortable with what had passed between them? She wanted to set his mind at ease and return things to the way they had been before.

"Okay." He scooted out of the kitchen without looking at her. She was about to follow him when she heard the whinny of a horse outside. She looked out the window. It wasn't the bishop. It was Danny with his sister Eva and Annabeth.

Her daughter jumped down from the buggy and came running into the house. "I don't see his car. Is Tully still here?" she asked with a worried expression.

"He's having a game of checkers with Gideon."

"Oh, *goot*." Annabeth sighed loudly with relief. "I was afraid he had gone. How is Diamond?"

"You should go and get a report from Tully. The vet was just here."

Eva and Danny came through the door as Annabeth went charging down the hall. Eva shook her head. "I have never seen that child so energetic. The whole school year she has been as shy as a mouse. I thought giving her a big part in the school play might bring her out of her shell, but I never expected her to pop out like a jack-in-the-box."

"All she has talked about all day long is her cowboy friend," Danny said. "I can't wait to meet him."

"He and Gideon are engaged in a game of checkers in Gideon's room." She kept her smile in place and tried to give the appearance of a calm, in-control woman.

Eva pulled off her gloves and traveling bonnet. She straightened her *kapp*. "I'm eager to meet this paragon, as well."

"Tully is hardly a paragon, but Annabeth has met so few outsiders that he seems larger-than-life to her.

Danny, did you have a chance to tell the bishop we needed to see him?"

He hung up his hat. "I did. He should be here soon."

She couldn't think of another reason to stall. She was going to have to face Tully sooner or later. "Well, come and visit with Gideon for a bit and cheer him up. He is depressed at being forced into bed rest, as you can imagine."

She led the way down the hall. As she reached for the doorknob, she heard an explosion of laughter from inside the room. She opened the door. Annabeth was giggling as she sat on the end of the bed clapping her hands. "He beat you, *Daadi*."

Gideon was howling with laughter. "You did not just do that!"

Tully chuckled as he leaned back in his chair with a wide grin on his face and crossed his arms. "I told you I was good at checkers."

"Twelve moves—that's all it took on his part. I can't believe it." Gideon guffawed and slapped his thigh. It happened to be his bad leg, and he grimaced. "Oh, look what you made me do."

Danny leaned close to Becca's ear. "So very depressed."

It wasn't the scene she had been expecting. She was sure Gideon would be grumping about having to stay in bed, but he sounded and looked more cheerful than he had in months.

"*Mamm*, you should have seen *Daadi*'s face when Tully took his last two kings. It was so funny."

"I heard."

Danny crossed the room and held out his hand to Tully. "I'm Danny Coblentz. This is my sister Eva. She is Annabeth's teacher, and I am a teacher in training."

Tully surged to his feet and shook Danny's hand. "Mighty pleased to meet you folks," he said in his thickest drawl.

"Annabeth has been telling us all day about the cowboy that is staying at her house."

"I grew up on a ranch in Oklahoma, but I don't do much cowboying these days."

"What do you do?" Danny asked.

"A little bit of everything. I'm between jobs right now, so you can imagine that I was plumb tickled pink when Becca and Gideon asked me to stay on and help the family. Especially since I'm responsible for injuring their new calf."

"What did the veterinarian have to say?" Becca asked, as if relying on Tully's information was something she was used to doing. She saw Gideon's eyebrows rise, but thankfully he held his tongue.

"He was happy with the way the cast is holding up. Much of the swelling has gone down in her leg. He was really pleased that she was up and nursing. He said he would be back in two weeks to replace the cast. If there's more swelling or discoloration of the skin below the cast, I'm to call him right away. I added his number to my phone."

"All good news, then. You must show me how to beat Gideon at checkers. I've never bested him."

He met her gaze and smiled. There was nothing in his expression to suggest he was shaken by their encounter. She relaxed and pushed the troubling episode to the back of her mind.

Tully had his emotions well in hand as he gazed at Becca. Although he had been surprised by the intensity of his reaction to holding her hand, he wasn't going to make her uncomfortable with unwanted attention. Yes, he'd thought about kissing her, but what right did he have to even think such a thing? She was way out of his league. It was best to pretend those few stunned moments had never happened.

He could manage to be the jovial cowboy for a few weeks. He was used to pretending things were okay even when they weren't. Just like he could deny he wanted a drink when he did. Like right now.

Except that would be more than a relapse on his part. It would be a betrayal of Becca's trust. He couldn't do that. So he was going to smile and pretend he was fine.

"Something smells *goot*," Gideon said.

"Oh! My cakes! I almost forgot them." Becca spun around and hurried out of the room with the ribbons of her white bonnet fluttering behind her.

Tully turned to Eva, knowing she was a teacher. He figured she wasn't likely to be upset by his questions. "I'm sorry to say I know next to nothing about the Amish, but I'd like to learn more. What's that thing you Amish women wear on your heads called?"

"It's simply called a *kapp* or prayer covering."

"I hope you don't mind my asking, but why do you wear it?"

"It is a mark of our faith, but also because the Bible tells us we should cover our heads when we pray, and we may want to pray many times during the day. So it's best to always wear something."

"I see." It made sense when she explained it that way.

"We also use them to cover our hair," she added, "We believe only God and our husband should see our unbound tresses."

"Amish women never cut their hair," Danny said.

Tully nodded as the image of his grandmother fixing her hair each morning came to mind. "My grandmother never cut her hair. She always wore it braided, folded up and pinned to the back of her head. She told me once that her hair represented her thoughts and wearing it loose would lead to scattered thinking."

If Becca had never cut her hair, it had to be past her knees by now. He tried to imagine how it would look if she wore it down. Would it be like a long, rippling cape of red and gold? Just as quickly he dismissed the thought. He wasn't her husband.

"I'm sure Gideon or Becca will be happy to answer your questions about our Amish faith," Eva said.

Gideon nodded. "Indeed I will, but only after a re-match. You won't take me so easily this time."

Annabeth sat up straight. "You can ask me, too."

Tully chuckled. "Thanks, kiddo. I appreciate that."

She grinned at him. "Tell Eva and Danny about your mean pony. Tully is a *goot* storyteller."

"Maybe you should go and see if your mother needs any help in the kitchen first," he suggested.

"Okay." She hopped off the bed and went running down the hall.

He looked at Gideon. "She is a sweet kid."

"She is like her mother."

Tully shook his head. "Maybe Becca used to be that sweet, but that was before she got bossy."

Danny laughed. "You are right about that."

Eva rolled her eyes at her brother. "A man who gives orders is in charge. A woman who gives the same orders is bossy."

Tully held his hands up in surrender. "I stand corrected by the teacher."

The door opened, and Becca came in with several plates in her hand. Each one held a generous slice of streusel coffee cake. Tully moved the checkerboard from the table beside Gideon's bed and accepted a plate from her. He held it close to his nose and sniffed the wonderful aroma of caramelized cinnamon and brown sugar. "Umm, this smells delicious." He looked at Danny and pointed to the cake. "This is why I'm staying here. The woman can cook."

Danny smiled at Becca. "A *goot* thing for a single man to know about a single woman."

Tully glanced quickly between Danny and Becca. Was Danny implying that he was interested in Becca? Was she interested in him? If she was, it made it that much more important for Tully to keep a lid on his feelings for her.

Becca smiled demurely and left the room. Tully saw it as his chance to gain a little more information about their relationship. "Are the two of you a couple?"

Danny shook his head. His sister grinned at him and then at Tully. "My brother has high hopes that the situation will change."

Gideon adjusted his position in the bed. "My daughter-in-law claims she's not ready to marry again, but it would be *goot* for her, and for Annabeth, to have a man around the house who isn't an old cripple."

"I'm not in any hurry," Danny said. "I can wait until she is ready."

Tully was glad to know the lay of the land. It would help him ignore his attraction to Becca now that he knew there was someone waiting to step up and take care of her. Someone who wasn't an alcoholic ex-soldier and down-and-out cowboy.

Danny fixed his eyes on Tully. "I offered to come do the chores with her, but she said she already had a man to help."

Was that the reason Becca had suddenly changed her mind about letting him stay? "It's fortunate I was able to give her a hand."

Becca and Annabeth came back in with plates for Danny and Eva. "There is more if someone wants seconds."

Eva turned and looked out the window behind her. "I believe that is the bishop arriving."

Danny kept his attention on Tully. "I hope he approves of your staying here."

"You mean he might not?" Tully looked at Gideon. "I don't want to cause trouble for you and your family."

Gideon waved away his concern. "Elmer Schultz is a reasonable man. He will not object, but I would like to visit with him in private."

Eva and Danny nodded. Becca looked at her guests. "We can retreat to the kitchen."

"We should be leaving," Eva said. "We have so much work to do to get ready for our Christmas Eve production. I've never put on a school program before. I'm worried the parents will think I have done a poor job."

"Nonsense," Becca said. "From everything that Annabeth tells me, I'm sure your program will be a complete success."

"If the Yoder twins behave and don't shoot paper wads at the back of our heads like they did today," Annabeth said in disgust.

Danny patted her shoulder. "I will keep a closer eye on the twins from now on. They won't cause any more trouble."

"We hope and pray," Eva added.

The group followed Becca to the kitchen. Tully hung back as everyone greeted the bishop when he came in. He was an imposing man in his midfifties with a shaggy gray-and-black beard that reached to the middle of his chest. He wore a flat-topped felt hat that looked identical to the ones Gideon and Danny had hung on the pegs near the door. Tully's gray cowboy hat was the only one that wasn't black.

The bishop caught sight of Tully right away. His short haircut, Western-style shirt and blue jeans set him apart from the somber dress favored by the Amish.

Becca introduced him. "Bishop Schultz, this is Tully Lange. He has agreed to work for us until Gideon is recovered."

"Are you new to this area?" the bishop asked, looking Tully up and down.

"I'm just sort of passing through."

The bishop's eyebrows rose at that, but he didn't comment.

"Thank you for the coffee cake, Becca," Eva said. "Annabeth, did you tell your mother about the party?"

Annabeth shook her head. "I forgot. I'm sorry."

"That's all right," Eva said in a tender tone. "You have had a busy day. Becca, I am supposed to tell you that Dinah and Leroy Lapp are hosting a Christmas cookie exchange the Saturday before Christmas. You and your family are invited, of course."

"That sounds like fun. Annabeth and I will be there. I hope Gideon is up to coming by then." Becca went to the door.

Danny stopped beside her. "Don't worry about fetching Annabeth after school. Eva or I will be happy to bring her home this week."

"I would be grateful. *Danki*." The brother and sister went out. Becca closed the door behind them.

Annabeth got her coat down. "May I go visit Diamond?"

Becca nodded. After the child left, the bishop looked at Becca. "Have you written to your grandfather about this? Samuel will want to return from Pennsylvania to help you."

"I will write soon, but his brother in Bird-in-Hand is dying. I don't want to burden Samuel with this news yet when I have all the help I need."

"I understand. I would see Gideon now."

She gave a slight bow of her head and went down the hall ahead of him. Tully was helping himself to coffee from the pot on the back stove when she returned.

He held out the cup he had just filled. "Would you like some?"

"I would, *danki*." She took it from him and sat at the table.

He filled another cup for himself and sat across from her. "It's been quite a day."

She sighed heavily. "It has."

"I like Annabeth's teacher."

Becca smiled softly. "Eva is a good woman. She cares for the children as if they are her own. Three of them will be after the wedding. She is marrying our blacksmith, Willis Gingrich."

He hesitated but couldn't resist learning more about her relationship with Danny. "Her brother seems like a nice guy."

"He is." She stirred a small amount of sugar into her coffee.

Tully tried to read her expression, but she wouldn't look at him. "He seems to like you a lot."

"We are friends."

"Just friends? I get the feeling that he wants to be more than that."

She glared at Tully. "Then he will have to learn to live with disappointment."

"Sorry, didn't realize it was a touchy subject."

"It is a closed subject."

He held up one hand. "Got it. Now what?"

"We still have the evening milking to do."

He flexed his sore fingers, took a sip of coffee and started to rise. "I'll get started on that."

"Finish your coffee first."

He sank back onto the chair. "Are you worried about what your bishop will say?"

"A little."

"Can he refuse to help pay the hospital bill?"

"He won't. If Gideon had been hurt doing something that went against our *Ordnung*, he could, but not for a simple accident."

"*Ordnung*, that means 'order.' If he did something against the order?"

"*Ja*, the *Ordnung* is like the rules of our church."

"What would be against the rules?"

"If Gideon had been driving a car or a snowmobile, doing something that isn't permitted."

"Do you have a lot of rules?"

"We have exactly enough," she said with a little smile.

"Who makes them? The bishop?"

"They aren't a set of written rules. They are the way we are expected to live our lives. The way we dress, the way we treat each other, the way we worship. I think in the same manner you learned to be a cowboy, our children learn to be Amish. Certain things are understood and expected. We wear plain-colored clothing. We don't use electricity in our homes. Our women wear *kapps*, and the men wear black hats in the winter and to prayer services but straw hats for working in the summer."

"You mean like a cowboy has a hat for work and a better one to wear when he goes to church?"

"*Ja*, I think so. We do get more specific. Each church group decides things like the style of *kapp* the women will wear and the size of the band around the men's hats."

"Why does it matter how wide a man's hatband is?"

"It helps us identify each other. If I see a woman with a heart-shaped *kapp*, I know she is from Lancaster. The same goes for the men's hats."

"Do the rules ever change?"

"Most have been the same for generations, but twice each year the entire congregation of baptized members can agree to a change. This church voted to allow propane furnaces and appliances several years ago. Other Amish use only wood to heat their homes, while still others allow solar power. As I told you, I have lived in many different places. In Kansas the Amish farmers use tractors instead of horses as we do here. We may all be Amish, but we aren't the same."

"Interesting." It seemed the Amish were more diverse than he first thought.

She tipped her head slightly as she regarded him. "Is it?"

He nodded. "It is. I've never known much about the Amish. I'm happy to lessen my ignorance."

"I'm pleased by your desire to understand us. Not everyone wants to make the effort."

"Do you mean the locals?"

"Here?" She shook her head. "We have been welcomed in this community. This area has been home to family potato farms for generations, but many of their young people have moved away looking for what they believe are better opportunities. Older farmers know the land they have spent a lifetime caring for will pass out of the family when they are gone. But they see us, using horses to plant and harvest, holding tight to our faith, our families and community the way their parents and grandparents did, and they like what they see. Many have sold their land to us rather than see it gobbled up by big commercial farms who can pay more than we can afford."

"You make it sound like a slice of paradise."

"Paradise is what we strive to obtain after this life. What we seek here is hard work, food for our bodies, *goot* friends and a loving family."

"Still sounds a bit like paradise, except for the hard work part. Which I know is waiting in the barn for me, so I will take my leave of you."

"I will be out after the bishop leaves."

"I might be done by then."

"Ten cows milked by you alone?" She leaned back in her chair and crossed her arms. "I don't think so."

He put on his fleece-lined jean jacket and settled his cowboy hat on his head. "Be careful. Gideon didn't think I could beat him at checkers, either." He ran his fingers around the brim of his hat in a salute and went out the door.

Chapter Seven

Tully wasn't done milking by the time Becca came out that evening. Thankfully the bishop came to the barn with her to help finish the job. He even took the milk to the collection station in the back of his buggy.

Afterward, Tully climbed the steel ladder into the tall concrete block silo and pitchforked out several hundred pounds of silage to fill the waiting feed cart below. Annabeth then drove the docile draft horse down the center aisle of the barn while Becca and Tully shoveled the silage into the feed bunks on either side. By the time they finished the chores, it was dark and snowing heavily.

Tully collapsed onto a kitchen chair, feeling more worn out than he had been since boot camp. Becca got busy putting together their supper. He barely had enough energy to eat it. Afterward, he poked his head in to see how Gideon was getting along on his way to his own bed.

Gideon was reading by the light of an oil lamp. He closed the book. "How are my cows?"

"Milked and fed. That's all I can say."

"Are any of them off their feed? Did you check the

ones you milked for cracked teats or signs of infection? Never mind. I should go check them myself. Hand me my crutches." He pointed to them beside the door.

"Becca would know if there was anything wrong. She's bringing your supper. Ask her. I'm going to bed and I may never get up again."

"Not so easy to milk ten cows by hand, is it, Cowboy?"

"No comment."

Tully continued down the hall with the sound of Gideon's mirth following him. He pulled off his boots and crawled under the covers without taking off his clothes. It seemed like only a few minutes later that Annabeth was nudging his shoulder.

"Tully, *Mamm* says it's time to get up."

He opened one eye. It was still dark outside the window. "It can't be."

He closed his eye again. Everything hurt. His arms hurt, his shoulders hurt and especially his hands. They ached like he had broken bones.

Annabeth shook him once more. "*Mamm* says to get up or she will pour water on your head."

"She wouldn't dare," he muttered.

"Are you sure about that? I have a glass in my hand," Becca said from his doorway.

Merciless woman. "I'm up. I'm up. Go away."

"If you aren't in the kitchen in five minutes, I will be back. Come on, Annabeth. We will see if we have gotten a bargain in our hired man or not."

"I never said I was a bargain, I said I worked cheap. For room and board. Which means something to eat and a place to sleep!" he shouted at the closed door.

He sat up in the cold room and shivered. This was

too much like his unheated second-story bedroom back on the ranch when he was a kid. He used to scrape frost off the windows in the winter with his fingernails. He shot a glance at the window. Yup, lots of frost.

He grabbed his boots and hurried to the kitchen, where Becca had the wood-burning oven door open, beating back the chill. He stood in front of it slowly turning around to warm all sides.

"Your room was a little chilly this morning."

"A little?"

She chuckled softly. "You might want to open the heating vent."

"There's heat? Now you tell me."

"*Ja*, we have a propane furnace. I keep the room closed off when no one is using it. I forgot to open it yesterday. The coffee is ready. When you're done roasting yourself and have had some, meet me in the barn."

How could she be so chipper this early in the morning? She was putting him to shame. He couldn't let a little slip of a woman like Becca make him look bad. "No point thawing out if I'm going outside."

He glanced at her face. She was struggling not to laugh at him as she handed him a cup. "Wear Gideon's overcoat and muck boots. We had about six inches of snow last night."

"*Wunderbar!*" He poured himself a half cup of hot coffee, added enough water to cool it and downed it in two gulps. He set his cup on the table.

Annabeth balanced a full cup on a saucer as she walked toward the hall. "I'm taking this to *Daadi*."

"Tell him I hope he gets well real soon. Real soon."

"I will." She smiled brightly, not catching on to the sarcasm in his voice.

He saw it was still snowing when he opened the door. He pulled his hat low on his brow and trudged across the farmyard, following Becca's tracks to the barn. Inside, he saw the glow of her lantern by Rosie and Diamond's stall. He walked over to lean on the gate. She was checking the calf's leg.

"How is she?"

Becca looked up. "Fine, I think. The leg is warm. The swelling is a little better. She was nursing when I came in, so she seems to be getting around on it."

"That's good news."

The calf moved away from her. It came to reach between the boards and nuzzle Tully's knee. He scratched her head. "Did you miss me last night?"

Becca came to stand beside him and patted the calf's back. "I believe she did. She has bonded to you."

He crouched to rub the calf under her chin. "I'm the one who almost ran you over."

"I think she has forgiven you for that."

"I hope so." He stood up. "I should get started milking. You're twice as fast as I am, but I will do half of them even if it takes longer so you can get Annabeth to school."

"As you wish." She handed him two clean pails and went down to the milking stanchions, where she lit a second lantern.

Tully couldn't believe how sore the muscles in his forearms were. He hoped he could work the stiffness out of them, but it didn't take long to prove that wasn't going to happen. Becca finished her half of the cows and left. He was working on his third cow when someone blocked the light. "I'll take over, *Englisch*."

He looked up to see an unfamiliar Amish man holding out his hand for Tully's pail. The man was younger than he was, tall, blond and he didn't have a beard. "Who are you?"

"Gabriel Fisher, but most folks call me Gabe. These are my *brudders*, Asher and Seth." Two men walked past Tully, each with a milk pail in their hands. One looked identical to Gabe.

Tully might have sore muscles and aching hands, but he wasn't about to admit he couldn't do the job. "I'm fine. I'll finish here."

"We can't both milk the same cow," Gabe said, nudging Tully with his knee.

Tully stood. Gabe took the bucket out of his hands. *"Danki."*

Tully stepped back. The man sat down on the milking stool and got to work.

Tully frowned. "I'll go fill the feed cart."

"Moses is doing that," Gabe said without looking up.

"Who is Moses?"

"Our baby *brudder*," one of the others said.

Gabe looked up at Tully. "Go get your breakfast."

Tully couldn't think of an argument. He rubbed his aching arms and walked up to the house just as Becca drove in. She had done half the milking and taken her child to school before he had finished a quarter of the morning's work. He wasn't proving to be much help to her.

He held the horse's bridle as she got down from the buggy. "You didn't have to call in the cavalry. I would've gotten everything done."

"What are you talking about?"

"The Fisher brothers are in the barn doing the chores for me."

"Are they? How kind of them. The bishop must've told them we needed help."

"You didn't ask them to come this morning?"

"*Nee*, I took Annabeth to school and came straight home. I spoke to Danny but no one else."

"Oh."

"You sound disappointed that the brothers are here."

"I wanted to do it myself." To accomplish something that helped her.

She chuckled. "That was not the impression you gave me this morning."

He followed her into the house. "Maybe I'm a slow starter, but I can pull my weight. You hired me to do a job. I intend to do it."

She took off her coat and large black bonnet. "Do not worry, Tully Lange, there is much more work for you. Sit. I will fix your breakfast."

He reluctantly sat down. It was humiliating to realize how little help he had provided to the hardworking family.

Another failed job. All he had really done was give Becca one more mouth to feed. Maybe it would be better if he left.

He looked so much like a pouting little boy that Becca wanted to laugh and ruffle his hair. She didn't. She didn't want him to think she was making fun of him. It was easy to see he was feeling low. She patted his shoulder. "You will get faster."

"Sure." He didn't sound convinced.

"How do you want your eggs?"

"Scrambled. I can cook for myself if you have other things to do."

"Do not worry about making more work for me. I like to cook. Shall I mix some sausage in with your eggs?"

"That sounds good. How is Gideon this morning?"

"Fussy. Grumpy. Pretty much the same as he is every day except when Annabeth is around."

"It's easy to see that he dotes on her. She's a cute kid."

"Have you any children?" He had never said if he was married or not. Becca cracked the eggs into the skillet.

"Nope. No wife or kids."

She glanced at him over her shoulder. "Why not?"

He looked surprised. "Why haven't I married? Oh, all the usual excuses. Never found the right woman. It never seemed like the time for me to settle down."

"But you would like to have a family, wouldn't you?" She tried to imagine him as a father with a little dark-haired boy at his side wearing boots and a cowboy hat, standing with his hip cocked and his thumbs hooked in his belt.

"Someday, I guess. When I have my life in order. I'd need a job and a place to live, for starters."

"Do you still have family in Oklahoma?"

"My grandparents raised me. They are both gone. The ranch went to my uncle. He and I never got along. He's an attorney in Tulsa. He sold the place as quickly as he could."

"That must have been sad for you. What about your parents? Where are they?"

"I have no idea."

She turned away from the stove to gape at him. "You have no idea where your parents are?"

"My mother left me with her folks when I was a few days old. She never came back. I must have been one *ugly* baby," he said with a broad grin.

"I see no humor in your story."

"If I don't laugh about it, I'm liable to cry."

She sat down at the table across from him. "There is no shame in our tears."

He shrugged. "I don't normally talk about that part of my life. My grandmother thought the man my mother ran off with was my father but never knew for sure. It was hard growing up knowing my own mother didn't want me, but I got over it. I haven't thought about her in a long time." He fell silent again.

He seemed to be miles away. Becca waited for him to speak. Finally he drew a deep breath. "When I was a kid, I always hoped she would come back, you know. To see how I turned out, maybe even say she was sorry for dumping me with my grandparents, but she never did."

Becca went back to the stove and stirred the eggs. It was difficult to imagine a mother leaving her baby and never returning. While the tone of Tully's voice was casual, she knew his mother's actions must have caused him great pain. "Have you forgiven her?"

"I guess so. I can't know what her life was like. She might've had a good reason for doing what she did. I thought about trying to track her down. It would be nice to know if I had brothers and sisters somewhere."

"Family is very important to us. Many Amish families have three or four generations living on the same farm, even in the same house."

"That isn't the way most folks do it, but if it works for you, more power to ya."

He grimaced and rolled his shoulders back as she

dished the eggs and sausage onto his plate. "Who knew milking cows was such hard work?"

"Everyone who has milked them by hand." She pulled out a pan of biscuits she had kept warming in the oven and set them on the table. She sat down with a cup of coffee.

"It sure explains why getting your milk at the grocery store caught on." He began eating and soon cleaned his plate, plus three of her biscuits loaded with butter and her homemade peach jam.

He sat back with a satisfied sigh. "That was delicious. *Danki.*"

She inclined her head. *"Du bischt wilkumm."*

"That means 'you're welcome'?"

"It does."

She reached for his plate, but he held it away from her. "I will take care of this. It's the least I can do."

"Danki."

"Du bischt wilkumm, Frau Beachy," he said smugly and carried the plate to the sink.

"Sis kald heit, ja?"

He frowned slightly. "I understood 'cold' in that sentence, but what is cold?"

"Not so *goot* is your *Deitsh.*"

He turned around and leaned his arms on the counter behind him. "Then teach me."

Did he mean that? "I said it is cold today."

"Sis kald heit." He pointed to the coffeepot. "Coffee."

"Kaffee."

He pointed to the door. *"Tur."*

She shook her head. *"Nee,* is *deah."*

"That's crazy. I wonder why the difference if the Amish came from Germany originally?"

"I don't know."

He pointed to his waist. "What's this?"

"Belt."

"I know it's my belt. How do you say it in Deitsh?"

She leaned toward him. "Watch my lips closely. Belt."

"Very funny." He patted his head. *"Kopf."*

"Ab en kopp," she said with a chuckle as the outside door opened. The Fisher brothers filed in with a blast of cold air.

The three eldest brothers were triplets, but only two of them, Gabe and Seth, were identical tall blond men with bright blue eyes. Asher had brown hair and dark eyes. He looked more like Moses, the youngest brother.

Gabe took off his hat. "We have finished the milking, fed the animals and cleaned the stalls. We have loaded the milk cans on your wagon. We'll deliver them for you."

"I appreciate that." Becca gestured to Tully. "This is Tully Lange, who is helping us until Gideon gets well. These are the Fishers. They are wheelwrights and buggy makers and new to the community, like us."

"Nice to meet you," Tully said without sounding sincere.

Gabe nodded to him. "If that's all, we'll be back this evening."

Tully straightened. "You don't need to do that. I can manage."

"Da Englisch ist ab en kopp right enough," Gabe said with a big grin. His brothers all chuckled.

Tully looked at her suspiciously. "What's wrong with my head?"

"Nothing." She tried to appear innocent.

Tully looked at Gabe. "What did she say earlier?"

"She said you are off in the head, *Englisch*. A fellow in his right mind wouldn't want to milk all those cows by himself. We will be back tonight and tomorrow, but not all of us. I'm afraid we won't be able to help for long. We have two cousins getting married in Pennsylvania, and we'll be attending the weddings next week. See you later." He held out his hand, only to jerk it away before Tully could shake it.

"I don't want to risk hurting those tender fingers. You will need them." Gabe chuckled as he put his hat on. His brothers followed him out the door.

"Funny man," Tully muttered, crossing his arms over his chest.

"Gabe is well-known for his sense of humor."

"You have the same problem, *Frau* Beachy. *Ab en kopp*," he muttered in mock disgust.

"It's not a problem, *Englisch*. It's a gift."

She caught the sparkle of mirth in his eyes and was happy his glumness had vanished. He tried to keep a straight face but started chuckling. It was contagious. Soon they were both doubled over with laughter.

He was a man who could take a joke and laugh at himself. She liked that about him. "I'm glad you decided to remain with us, Tully Lange," she said, realizing how much she meant it. He might not be the best farmhand, but there was something about him that made her want to smile.

"Thanks. I reckon I'll stay on a few more days and see if I can get the hang of being a dairyman."

She stopped smiling. "Were you thinking of leaving sooner?"

"It crossed my mind. I'm not exactly *goot* help."

"Do not be so hard on yourself."

"Guess it's a force of habit. I'll go see if Gideon is ready for our checkers rematch."

"He will enjoy that, but maybe let him win one game."

"Can't do that. It would make him mad if he thought I wasn't playing my best. He wants to win fair and square. I'm the same way. What other work do you have for me?"

"The milk room needs to be washed down and the equipment cleaned with hot water, soap and bleach. I'll get the water heating for that. The wood box outside is getting low. Oh, and the wheels on the buggy need to be greased."

"Got it. Anything else?"

"That's enough for one morning. Go enjoy your game with Gideon."

He flexed his fingers. "I hope I can pick up a checker. Gideon might have to move his pieces and mine."

"I have something that might help." She turned to the cabinet where she kept her ointments and medical supplies. She found the bottle she was looking for and carried it to him.

"Give me your hand."

He did, and she poured some of the oil into his palm. He sniffed. "What is it?"

"A little cayenne pepper in olive oil. Rub it in well, but be careful not to touch your mouth or your eyes." She realized how close she was standing to him and how natural it felt to look up and see him smiling at her. His smile faded, and his eyes darkened.

What did he see when he looked at her so intently? She wanted to ask, but she was afraid of the answer.

"I can't remember the last time someone wanted to take care of me. You're a good woman, Becca," he said softly. "Thank you."

"You're welcome." Her voice sounded breathless to her own ears. He stirred her in ways she had thought she had buried with her husband.

The sound of Gideon's crutches thumping down the hallway caused them to move apart. She stepped to the stove, opened the firebox and started adding wood. Tully rubbed his hands together, spreading the oil over them. Gideon came slowly into the kitchen with a look of intense concentration on his face.

"You shouldn't be up yet," Becca said sharply.

"I can't stay in that bed another minute. What are the two of you doing?"

"Nothing," they said together and then exchanged guilty glances.

Gideon arched one eyebrow as he glanced between them. Becca closed the firebox and banged the lid back into place.

Tully flexed his fingers. "This is getting pretty hot."

"What is it?" Gideon asked.

"Some of the rub I make for your hip. You will have to wash that off before you milk tonight," she said, indicating Tully's hands.

A grin tugged at the corner of his mouth. "Or not. That might make for an interesting show."

She shook her head at his foolishness. "You mean seeing how far a cow can kick a grown man? It would only be funny for the onlookers."

Gideon chuckled. "Let me know when you try it so I can sell tickets."

"I may sell tickets to our next checkers game instead

so everyone can watch you getting whomped by me again. Are you up to a game today?"

"What is whomped?"

"Beaten, badly."

"There will be no whomping done by you. I know your tricks now."

"Ha! You know some of them."

"Go get the board. We will see your pride go before your fall."

"My fall? Not a chance." He walked down the hallway to get the game.

Gideon gave a little laugh. "I like that fellow even if he is a boaster."

"I like him, too. He makes me smile, thinking about the nonsense he utters."

"I will enjoy having him around for a few weeks." Gideon slanted a glance in her direction. "He will brighten our Christmas season, but he will be gone after that."

Was Gideon giving her a gentle reminder of that fact? He didn't need to. It was always in the back of her mind. She could like Tully, but not too much. He didn't belong among them. He was an outsider who was simply passing through their little corner of the world. He would get in his car and drive away, leaving her behind to resume her sad, lonely life.

She straightened her shoulders. That wasn't right. She had Annabeth, Gideon and many friends in New Covenant. She wasn't sad, but sometimes she did get lonely. A man like Tully Lange might ease that ache for a short time when he made her laugh, but he wasn't the answer for her. She must guard her heart against caring too much.

Chapter Eight

The following morning Tully opened his eyes when there was a knock on his door. "Tully, are you awake?" Becca asked.

"I'm up," he said, wishing there was some part of him that didn't hurt. If the cows had run over him one by one, he figured he would feel about the same. It was starting out to be a bad day. At least it wasn't as cold in the room with the small heating vent open.

He sat up on the side of the bed, rubbed his face and sighed heavily. He had a choice to make. Head on to Caribou and forget about the pretty Amish widow and her family or tough it out and become useful. It'd been a while since he had been useful even to himself.

He pushed to his feet, wondering if he could do it. Could he really make a difference and become something other than a liability for Becca?

In the kitchen she handed him the clean pails. "How are you?"

She barely looked at him. Her demeanor was cool. What was up? "It's too early to tell," he muttered, reaching for Gideon's overcoat.

Becca shook her head. "You do not need to stay with us. We can manage." She looked at him then. "I thank you for all you've done so far."

This was his chance to bow out gracefully. Except when he looked into her weary eyes, he realized he didn't want to leave. Not yet. "You can't get rid of me that easily."

"I'm not trying to get rid of you."

"Glad to hear it, because I surely do love your amazing cooking."

The smile he hoped to see tugged at the corner of her lips. "Flattery is not our way. I have told you this."

"Becca Beachy, your cooking is downright horrible. It could make a skunk gag." He leaned toward her and grinned. "Is that what you'd rather hear?"

She giggled as she stepped around him. It was a beautiful sound. "You know it is not, you foolish fellow." She flashed him a grin and reached for the doorknob.

In that instant he forgot about how much his arms ached and how tired he was. He could do one thing to brighten her day. He could make her laugh.

When she opened the door, the cold hit him full in the face, sending a shiver to the soles of his feet. As he followed her out into the dark and frigid morning, he called himself every kind of fool for choosing to stay for no other reason than to see her smile.

The barn was a welcome haven of warmth when he stepped inside out of the wind. They stopped to check on Diamond and Rosie first. He figured Annabeth would be waiting for a report when they came in. Rosie was lying down chewing her cud with her sleeping calf pressed close to her side. "They both look comfortable," he said.

"I agree. We won't disturb them until they are up."

Four of the cows had already moved from their bedding area to their milking stanchions on their own. Becca lit the second lantern hanging on the wall and took down her three-legged stool and a currycomb. "Don't try to rush just because the Fishers are coming. The cows will not appreciate it. They can sense your moods. A calm, happy cow gives more milk."

"In other words, I need to be a pleasant cowboy."

"Exactly." She walked back to the next cow in line.

Tully hung up his hat and took down his little seat and the remaining brush. "Which one is this?" he asked as he swept the loose dirt and bedding from the animal's back legs and udder.

"That is Dotty."

"I remember you, Dotty. You're the troublemaker."

The cow tossed her head and switched her tail. He patted her hip. "Prove me wrong and behave. There'll be an extra ration of grain for you if you do."

He heard a chuckle from Becca. "Bargaining with a cow? Is that how Oklahoma cowboys manage their herds?"

"We do whatever it takes." He sat down and got to work. In a few minutes, his stiff muscles began to limber up. Dotty shifted restlessly. He started singing to calm her. "Home, home on the range. Where Dotty and her friends can go play. Where never is heard a discouraging word and cowboys can sing songs all day."

He heard clapping from the front of the barn. He'd forgotten about the Fishers.

"*Goot* tune, *Englisch*. I can take over."

Tully thought it was Gabe looking over Dotty's back, but he couldn't be sure. "It's Cowboy to you, mister. Go find your own cow. This one is mine. Better yet, take over from Becca and let her go start breakfast. I'm getting hungry." She deserved a break from the hard work more than he did.

Gabe laughed and moved to her side. "You heard the cowboy."

"I did. The man thinks of nothing but his stomach."

She walked past with two full pails in her hands. Tully had only filled one. He settled into his work once more.

Tully learned Gabe and Moses were the only two brothers to come that morning. Moses had filled the wagon with silage and was waiting to get started feeding when they finished milking. Moses drove while Gabe and Tully shoveled the feed into the long troughs on both sides of the center aisle.

"Do you feed cattle this way where you are from, Cowboy?" Moses called over his shoulder.

"My family raised beef cattle, not dairy cows. We fed silage in the winter but from a grain wagon pulled by a tractor. In the summer the cattle were out on grass in huge pastures. I spent a lot of hours checking cattle and fences on horseback."

Gabe grinned at Tully. "Did you ever ride wild bucking horses?"

"Not on purpose."

Gabe's brow furrowed, then just as quickly his confusion cleared. He slapped Tully on the back. "Not on purpose. Ha! That's a *goot* one. Once *Mamm* decided to plow her garden because *Daed* hadn't gotten around to it. The plow horse spooked and jumped the fence while he was still harnessed to the plow. He pulled down a ten-foot section around *Mamm*'s garden. *Daed* asked if she had torn down the fence on purpose. Quick as can be, she said she wanted to put a gate there all along."

The brothers shared funny stories about their own experiences with horses that didn't go as planned. Tully was grinning from ear to ear when they were finished with the chores. The two reminded him of the ranch hands who had worked for his grandfather. Hardworking, humor-loving, loyal, dependable men. Were other Amish the same, or were the Fishers unique?

The brothers waved goodbye as they drove the wagon loaded with milk to the collection station, leaving Tully feeling that he had managed to improve their opinion of him and make two new friends in the process. Which was good because they had promised to return and help with the milking, and he needed the help.

Becca was at the stove when he came in. She cocked her head to the side. "Why the big smile?"

"Those Fisher brothers are a hoot. Are all Amish so funny?"

"Are all cowboys as funny as you?"

"Some, not all."

"It is the same with the Amish."

He patted his stomach. "What's for breakfast? And lunch? And supper?"

Annabeth came running into the room. "Tully, you're still here. I was worried."

He caught her up and lifted her to straddle his hip. "I'm not gonna leave without telling you goodbye, so don't worry."

"To worry is to doubt *Gott*," Becca said.

Tully deposited Annabeth on her chair. "See. No worrying from now on."

"Okay. Tell me a story."

"Nope. I'm gonna go help your grandpa get up. Stories will have to wait until after school."

"Aw."

He leaned down and whispered in her ear loud enough so Becca could hear him, too. "What did the duck say to the dog?"

"I don't know. What?"

Tully tweaked her nose. "Nothing, silly. Ducks can't talk."

He left the room with the sound of their giggles gladdening his heart. It wasn't turning out to be such a bad day after all.

The following morning Tully was already in the kitchen getting the fire going when Becca entered the room. She stopped short at the sight of him and grinned. He liked the way her eyes lit up when she smiled.

She set her hands on her hips. "You are up before me. I am impressed."

"Don't be. I happened to be hungry and got up looking for something to eat."

She chuckled. "You are a glutton."

He realized how different his life had become. Only a few months ago, his first thoughts in the morning had been where to find his next drink. A week ago it had been how he would avoid taking a drink. Now the first thing he wanted was to see Becca's smiling face. He hadn't thought about taking a drink all week.

He handed her two of the pails he had already scrubbed. She handed them back. "You and the Fishers can do the milking. I have work to do in the house."

"As long as it involves cooking, I'm fine with that." He slapped his hat on his head and went out.

Becca's smile faded as she realized it was impossible to harden her heart against the man. Every minute she spent in Tully's company was a joy. She was wise enough to know the path she was on would only lead to heartache. She simply didn't know how to step off it. He was going to leave one day soon, taking this strange joy with him, and then it wouldn't matter.

She fixed breakfast and then took Annabeth to school. Danny was waiting on the school steps, but she let Annabeth out and quickly drove away. She didn't want to speak to him or anyone.

She worked the rest of the day doing mending and sewing Annabeth's costume for the Christmas play in the little alcove off her bedroom. That way she avoided Tully's company. He kept Gideon entertained. She could hear them laughing in Gideon's room down the hall, and that made her smile. Tully was surely a godsend for her father-in-law.

When it was time for school to be over, she came out of her room. She hoped Eva would bring Annabeth home, but she hoped in vain. She and Tully were in the living room with Gideon when Danny came in. He nodded to Gideon. Annabeth went straight to Tully. "How is Diamond?"

He grinned at her. "Why don't we go out and check on her, unless your mom has chores for you to do."

Becca shook her head. "They can wait until you've seen your calf."

"Okay, come on, Tully." She darted to the door.

He gathered his hat and coat. "Wish I had your energy."

"Tell me another cowboy story, Tully."

"Let's see. Have I told you about the time I roped a coyote?"

"Nope. Is it a funny story?"

Tully chuckled. "It is now. Not so much when it was happening, though." He went out with her and closed the door.

Danny turned to Becca. "The child is overly fond of him."

Becca shrugged. "She likes his stories. I don't see the harm in her listening to him."

"I worry that he is making the outside world seem too attractive to her."

Gideon chuckled. "I hardly think a few cowboy stories will entice Annabeth to leave the Amish. She's only seven."

"Her hero worship isn't healthy," Danny said, giving Becca a pointed look.

Becca didn't care for his tone. "I know my child. If I see something to be concerned about, I will deal with it."

"I hope so. If you need help dealing with him, let me know."

"*Danki*, Danny, but I'm sure Gideon and I can manage." She folded her arms across her middle. "Goodbye."

He seemed to sense he'd stepped over the line. "I'll bring Annabeth home again tomorrow."

"That will be fine." She walked to the kitchen door and opened it.

He looked as if he wanted to say something else.

Becca narrowed her eyes at him. He wisely held his peace and left.

She returned to Gideon. "The nerve of that man."

"His concern is as much for you as for Annabeth."

"I'm not suffering from hero worship any more than you are."

"Aren't you?"

"I'm not." She left the room and retreated to her bedroom. She didn't slam the door, although she wanted to. She dropped to sit on her bed and rubbed her forehead. Was Danny right? Was Tully a bad influence on Annabeth?

He is a bad influence on me.

She needed to put an end to their growing friendship, but how? Should she tell him to leave?

Tully finished the morning chores with the help of only Moses on Friday. After the young man left, Tully walked into the house and stopped short in the doorway. Annabeth was seated at the kitchen table, crying, as Gideon and Becca looked on.

"What's going on?" He closed the door.

"They won't let me take you to school," she said and sobbed harder.

"Annabeth, calm down. This is not how we behave," Becca said sternly. She looked at Tully. "She has told her friends about you, but none of them believe you are a real cowboy."

"Maddie's brother Otto told me there aren't any cowboys in Maine," Annabeth said between sobs.

He crossed to where she sat and crouched beside her. "I'm sorry if they upset you."

"She is upset with me," Becca said. "I told her she

can't take you to show-and-tell today. It would be rude to ask you to be on display."

"Oh, I see. Your mom is right, Annabeth. I wouldn't like to be your show-and-tell exhibit." The idea of standing up in front of a schoolroom full of kids was enough to make his palms sweat. Being in front of the group had been one of the hardest parts of his therapy.

"But Jenny brought *bobbli* Eli."

Tully looked to Becca for an explanation. "Her sister's new baby," Becca said.

"Well, Annabeth, I can see how that would give you the idea to bring me. Becca, do you suppose it would be okay if I rode to school with you this morning so I could meet her friend?" Meeting another first grader wasn't intimidating. He could manage that.

Annabeth turned pleading eyes to her mother. "Could he, *Mamm*?"

Becca looked to Gideon. He nodded once. "If Tully wishes to meet your friends, that is fine, but you are not to boast to others about having him stay with us."

Tully rose to his feet and held his hands out to his sides. "I'm not someone special. I'm just a man who grew up in a different place. Where I come from, there were lots of cowboys. You would've been the unusual one, because there were no Amish folks where I lived."

"None at all?" she asked, drying her tears with her hands.

"Not a one. Have you been practicing your part for the Christmas program?"

The change of topic brought out a hint of a smile. "I have. *Mamm* listens to me every night."

"I'd like to hear you recite your lines. Would that be okay?"

She nodded eagerly. "I'll tell them to you on the way to school."

Gideon folded his hands on the tabletop. "Now that this crisis is over, let us have our breakfast in peace."

Tully took his place across from Annabeth and bowed his head. He glanced up once to find Becca gazing at him. She looked down as soon as their eyes met, but he thought he detected gratitude in her expression. It could be that he was finally becoming something other than a burden.

Tully was being kind to her daughter. A spot of warmth settled in the center of Becca's chest. He had no idea how much she appreciated his compassionate understanding. Annabeth was a sensitive child. Perhaps because she was an only child. Becca sometimes wondered if she was doing her daughter a disservice by not seeking to marry again. Perhaps she was selfish, but she didn't want Annabeth to think of another man as her father.

After they finished eating, Tully helped Gideon to his favorite chair in the living room and settled him with the newspaper and a book close at hand. Becca took several bricks she'd had warming in the oven out to the buggy. Tully and Annabeth came out of the house as she drove the buggy up to the gate. Her daughter was smiling at Tully with something close to adoration in her eyes.

Becca opened the buggy door. "Hurry, or these bricks will be cold before we get to school."

Tully lifted Annabeth into the buggy, climbed in behind her and shut the door. "*Sis kald heit.* Did I get that right?" he asked.

Get Up To 4 Free Books!

Dear Reader,

IT'S A FACT: if you answer 4 quick questions, we'll send you 4 FREE REWARDS from each series you try!

Try **Love Inspired® Romance Larger-Print** books and fall in love with inspirational romances that take you on an uplifting journey of faith, forgiveness and hope.

Try **Love Inspired® Suspense Larger-Print** books where courage and optimism unite in stories of faith and love in the face of danger.

Or **TRY BOTH!**

I'm not kidding you. As a leading publisher of women's fiction, we value your opinions... and your time. That's why we are prepared to reward you handsomely for completing our mini-survey. In fact, we have 4 Free Rewards for you, including 2 free books and 2 free gifts from each series you try!

Thank you for participating in our survey,

Pam Powers

www.ReaderService.com

To get your 4 FREE REWARDS:
Complete the survey below and return the insert today to receive up to 4 FREE BOOKS and FREE GIFTS guaranteed!

"4 for 4" MINI-SURVEY

1 Is reading one of your favorite hobbies?
☐ YES ☐ NO

2 Do you prefer to read instead of watch TV?
☐ YES ☐ NO

3 Do you read newspapers and magazines?
☐ YES ☐ NO

4 Do you enjoy trying new book series with FREE BOOKS?
☐ YES ☐ NO

Please send me my Free Rewards, consisting of **2 Free Books from each series I select** and **Free Mystery Gifts**. I understand that I am under no obligation to buy anything, as explained on the back of this card.

☐ **Love Inspired® Romance Larger-Print** (122/322 IDL GQ5X)
☐ **Love Inspired® Suspense Larger-Print** (107/307 IDL GQ5X)
☐ **Try Both** (122/322 & 107/307 IDL GQ6A)

FIRST NAME   LAST NAME

ADDRESS

APT.#   CITY

STATE/PROV.   ZIP/POSTAL CODE

EMAIL ☐ Please check this box if you would like to receive newsletters and promotional emails from Harlequin Enterprises ULC and its affiliates. You can unsubscribe anytime.

LI/SLI-520-MS20

HARLEQUIN READER SERVICE—Here's how it works:

Accepting your 2 free books and 2 free gifts (gifts valued at approximately $10.00 retail) places you under no obligation to buy anything. You may keep the books and gifts and return the shipping statement marked "cancel." If you do not cancel, approximately one month later we'll send you 6 more books from each series you have chosen, and bill you at our low, subscribers-only discount price. Love Inspired® Romance Larger-Print books and Love Inspired® Suspense Larger-Print books consist of 6 books each month and cost just $5.99 each in the U.S. or $6.24 each in Canada. That is a savings of at least 17% off the cover price. It's quite a bargain! Shipping and handling is just 50¢ per book in the U.S. and $1.25 per book in Canada*. You may return any shipment at our expense and cancel at any time — or you may continue to receive monthly shipments at our low, subscribers-only discount price plus shipping and handling. *Terms and prices subject to change without notice. Prices do not include sales taxes which will be charged (if applicable) based on your state or country of residence. Canadian residents will be charged applicable taxes. Offer not valid in Quebec. Books received may not be as shown. All orders subject to approval. Credit or debit balances in a customer's account(s) may be offset by any other outstanding balance owed by or to the customer. Please allow 3 to 4 weeks for delivery. Offer available while quantities last.

▲ If offer card is missing write to: Harlequin Reader Service, P.O. Box 1341, Buffalo, NY 14240-8531 or visit www.ReaderService.com ▲

BUSINESS REPLY MAIL
FIRST-CLASS MAIL   PERMIT NO. 717   BUFFALO, NY

POSTAGE WILL BE PAID BY ADDRESSEE

HARLEQUIN READER SERVICE
PO BOX 1341
BUFFALO NY 14240-8571

NO POSTAGE
NECESSARY
IF MAILED
IN THE
UNITED STATES

Becca nodded. "*Ja*, it is cold today. I'm impressed you remembered."

"I've always been good with languages. I studied Spanish in high school, along with football and girls. Then I learned German when I was in the service. Not that speaking another language has ever done me much good. Annabeth, what do you want for Christmas?"

She scowled at him. "What do you mean?"

"You must have some special gift you are hoping to find under your Christmas tree. Maybe a doll, a new dress or a game you like."

Becca cleared her throat. "We don't give our children presents at Christmas the way the *Englisch* do, and we don't decorate trees. We may add a few pine branches to the mantel, and we will hang the Christmas cards we receive on ribbons, but nothing more. For us Christmas Day is a solemn day to be spent in quiet reflection and prayer. We do gather to celebrate the season with others beforehand and after. We go visiting and enjoy parties. The children certainly inspire us with their hard work on their Christmas program. I guess you could say it is their gift to us."

"I was going to cut a tree for you. Good to know that won't be necessary. Okay, Annabeth, what is your favorite subject? Don't say recess."

Annabeth frowned at him. "Recess isn't a subject. I like reading. Teacher has lots of books that she brought to our school. I'm going to read them all someday."

"A worthy goal. Becca, what was your favorite subject in high school, and don't say boys."

"Boys aren't a subject, either," Annabeth said with a shake of her head.

He chuckled. "They will be when you get a little older. Well, Becca?"

She glanced his way and saw he was waiting for her answer. "I did not go to high school. Amish children only attend school through the eighth grade."

"No kidding? High school was mandatory where I'm from."

"The Amish were granted a religious exemption by the Supreme Court in 1972."

"Okay then, what was your favorite subject in grade school?"

That he took the information in stride without any of the usual *Englisch* comments about the benefits of higher education surprised her. "Why do you want to know?"

"Because I'm a curious fellow. I want to know more about you." He turned slightly and stretched his arm along the back of the seat.

His hand was resting behind her shoulder. If she leaned back a little, they would be touching. She straightened her posture to prevent any contact. "About me or about the Amish?"

"Both."

"*Mamm* liked reading the best, same as me," Annabeth said.

"I can believe that. You were going to recite your lines for the Christmas program for me."

Annabeth grinned and nodded. "'I'm a little shepherd girl, and no one will help me find the Christ child.'" She sat up and gazed straight ahead. "'Where is the new king? I want to see him, too. I heard the angels say he is in Bethlehem. Can you tell me where to find him?'"

"That's very good," Tully said.

"That's not all. I go to many houses and ask for him. 'Is the new king here? Where is the new king?'"

Tully grew solemn. "Doesn't anyone tell you?"

"The innkeeper's daughter tells me there is a baby in the stable. That's my friend Maddie. When I go to the stable, I can't see him because all the other shepherds are gathered around him. I try to get close, but I keep getting pushed aside."

Tully shook his head. "That's not right. Someone has to let the littlest shepherd girl see the baby. Who will help her?"

Annabeth grinned. "A very kind man. Joseph. He lifts me up to see the new king, and I say, 'He is so beautiful.' Then everyone sings 'Silent Night.'"

"That sounds like a great program. I wish I could see it, though I don't imagine you allow *Englisch* folks in the audience."

"We do, don't we, *Mamm*? Tully can come."

"Our *Englisch* friends are always welcome, but Tully may not be here then, Annabeth. He has other friends he will want to see for Christmas."

"But I want him to be there. Can't you stay, Tully?"

"I reckon I can stick around until after your program, Annabeth. Consider it my Christmas present to you. I sure look forward to seeing it."

"That will be *wunderbar*, won't it, *Mamm*?" Annabeth turned to Becca with a beaming smile on her face.

"*Ja*, it will be *wunderbar*." Becca caught Tully's gaze and nodded in gratitude. He seemed to truly care about her daughter's happiness. Her respect and affection for him grew.

It took a little over twenty minutes to cover the three miles into New Covenant. It wasn't a town in the sense of the ones she had grown up around. It was more a collection of Amish homes and businesses along a one-mile stretch of the county road.

"The farms along here appear prosperous," he said.

"What makes you say that?"

"The barns are painted, and the fences are, too. Where I'm from, you see a lot of barns covered in rusty tin. Our fences are mainly barbed wire and steel posts. What do they raise this far north?"

"Potatoes, mostly. This county is the largest producer of potatoes in the state. Our growing season is short, but the days are very long this far north."

"Now that you say potatoes, I remember that's what Arnie talked about. He hated harvesting potatoes."

"I get to work in the potato fields next year maybe," Annabeth said.

Becca smiled down at her but shook her head. "I think maybe the year after that."

"We get a whole two weeks off from school during the potato harvest," Annabeth said. "Otto told me he made lots of money last summer."

"A lot of the labor of gathering and sorting potatoes has to be done by hand. Many of the public schools let the older students off for several weeks during the harvest, because the farmers need the labor. They've done it that way for more than one hundred years in this area."

"What do folks do during the winter?"

"Most of the Amish have small businesses. Michael Shetler has a clock-repair shop. Our bishop builds garden sheds and now some tiny homes, since more *Englisch* seem to want them. Gideon and I have no such problem keeping occupied in the winter. Cows must be milked twice a day, 365 days of the year."

Annabeth scooted forward on the seat and pointed. "That's our school. It's brand-new."

"It's a very nice-looking school," Tully said, smiling at her.

"I think so, too," Annabeth said. "That's my friend Maddie." She pointed to where several children were playing on a swing set. "Her brother Willis is the blacksmith. He's going to marry my teacher, and then she won't be my teacher anymore. That makes me sad."

"Danny is going to be your new teacher," Becca reminded her. "You like Danny."

"I like him, but I like Teacher Eva better. She brings treats, and she always finds the best stories to read to us."

"I'm sure Danny will find good stories, too," Tully said with a slight smirk on his face. Becca shot him a behave-yourself look.

"I hope so." Annabeth sounded anything but hopeful. Tully chuckled softly.

Becca could only hope that Annabeth's friends didn't embarrass Tully with their questions. Eva would handle the situation with grace, but she wasn't quite so sure about Danny. He had made it plain he didn't care for Tully.

Becca turned the horse into the schoolyard and stopped beside the hitching rail out front with the other buggies. "We should let Eva know you have come with us, and then you can go meet Maddie."

She led Tully up the steps into the school as Annabeth ran off to join her friend on the swing set. Becca cast a covert glance at Tully's face. What would he think of their simple one-room school?

Eva came forward to greet them with a smile. "Annabeth insisted she was going to bring you to show-and-tell, but I told her it would be best to ask you first. I'm glad she convinced you. I'm sure the children will have many questions for you."

Tully whipped off his hat. Becca noticed he turned it around nervously in his hands.

"I'm not good at speaking in front of folks. I'm just here to meet a little girl named Maddie."

Eva looked disappointed, but she nodded. "I understand. I used to be terrified of getting up in front of the children, but since I'm the teacher, I persevered and now it's only a little intimidating."

Tully stopped spinning his hat. "I'm relieved you understand."

"I'll take you outside and introduce you to Maddie," Becca said.

Tully put his hat on, tipped it to Eva and followed Becca out the door. She stopped on the school steps. A dozen or more parents and their children were waiting in the schoolyard. She saw Danny at the back of the crowd.

Michael Shetler stepped forward. "Remember me?" he asked Tully.

"Sure. You were the blocker for our little cattle drive. What's going on?"

"Danny invited us to see a demonstration of your cowboy skills."

"Oh, he did?" Becca scowled at Danny. What was he up to?

Danny stepped forward with a coiled rope in his hand and held it toward Tully. "Annabeth has told us so much about you. I hope you don't mind showing us a few of your tricks."

Chapter Nine

Tully took the rope from Danny with a hand that was surprisingly steady considering there had to be close to three dozen people watching him. He hadn't held a lariat in ten years. Not since his uncle had sold Tully's horse, saddle and almost everything else his grandfather had given him before putting him on a bus and sending him to a boarding school in New Orleans. His uncle had claimed that Tully needed a more rounded education, when what he really needed was a home. It was an arrangement that hadn't worked for Tully. He took off on his own two months later.

He glanced at Becca. She looked worried. Was she concerned that he was going to make a fool of himself? Because he was pretty sure that's what Danny was hoping to see. He held on to the tail of the rope and tossed it out in front of him.

"Do you trip cattle with the rope?" Danny asked and chuckled.

"I'm sure there's more to the skill than that," Becca said.

Tully looked at her. If she was so eager to defend him, he couldn't let her down. He hoped.

"A lariat, or lasso as it is sometimes called, has to be coiled properly before a fellow can throw it." Tully began gathering the rope into even-size rings, flipping it to make it lie flat in his grip.

"I told you he was a real cowboy," he heard Anna-beth whisper to another little girl beside her. He looked over the schoolboys.

"Which one of you is Otto?"

One boy of about ten or so took a step forward. "I am."

He had the same defiant gleam in his eyes that Tully had worn like a badge through his childhood. Tully pulled in the last of the rope and started to shake out a loop. "The eye that the rope goes through is called a hondo. You don't hold it. You want to make a loop and hold on to the rope about an arm's length away from the hondo. We call this length the shaft or spoke. See how I've got my index finger pointing down the shaft where I'm holding both sections together? That is the key to controlling where the rope will go. And just so you know, Otto, there are cowboys in every state, including Maine. Bull riders, bronc riders, calf ropers—they're everywhere. Of course, the best cowboys are from Oklahoma, if you ask me. You want to step out there about ten feet?"

The boy crossed his arms over his chest. "Not really."

Tully chuckled. "Okay. How about you, Danny? Do you want to be my target?"

Danny shook his head. "I don't think so."

Becca walked out in front of the group with her chin held high. "Is this far enough?"

Bless her heart. It seemed one person had faith in

him, and that was enough. "Cover your face with your hands so the rope doesn't scratch you."

"I will do it," Danny said suddenly.

Tully shook his head. "Nope. You had your chance. The lady is willing, and I'm gonna oblige her." He shook a bigger loop, and after whirling it above his head a few times, he let it fly. The rope settled around Becca's shoulders. He pulled it tight.

"A working cowboy usually has a horse that knows how to keep the rope taut." He handed the end to Annabeth. "Don't let her get away."

"I won't." The child grinned from ear to ear.

"The cowboy gets off his horse and goes hand over hand down on the rope all the way to his prize," he said as he demonstrated on his way to Becca.

When he reached her, he rested his hands lightly on her shoulders before lifting the rope off. "Did I hurt you?" he asked quietly.

She pulled her hands away from her face. Her grin was as big as Annabeth's. "Not at all, but I didn't get to see you throw it."

He adored the sparkle in her eyes when she smiled. He pretty much adored everything about her.

"Do it again," someone called out. He had forgotten for a moment that they had a crowd watching them.

Becca's smile disappeared. She looked down and hurried to stand behind Eva.

Tully raised his hat to the onlookers and prayed his sore, stiff muscles would remember what they were supposed to do. He wasn't seventeen anymore. "Danny wants to see some of my tricks. Annabeth, you can let go now."

Tully coiled the line and shook out another loop.

Instead of whirling it over his head, he held it out to his side, making it larger and larger. When it was big enough and spinning at the right speed, he hopped through it and back. He felt it clip his heel, but it didn't catch. Okay, once was enough for that stunt. He heard gasps of appreciation from some of the children.

He kept the rope spinning and raised it over his head, where he was able to make it drop down to circle his knees and rise again. Feeling more confident, he began spinning a butterfly loop. He went through a half dozen more tricks then decided he had done enough and should stop before he messed up in a big way.

He motioned to Otto. "Want to learn to throw a lasso?"

The boy came forward eagerly this time. Tully showed him how to coil the rope, how to make a loop and how to twirl it. When the kid had the hang of it, Tully looked around for a target. "Aim for the seat of the teeter-totter."

To his surprise, Otto's loop fell exactly where he wanted it. "Good job. Now you can teach the other kids how to do it. But remember, a rope is a tool—it isn't a toy. It can hurt someone if you aren't careful. Don't go home and try roping your papa's milk cow. She might not take it too kindly. Understand?"

Otto nodded. "I do."

Tully was pleased to see the defiance had faded from the kid's eyes.

"Tell them the story about how you roped a wild coyote," Annabeth said.

Tully shook his head. "I'll leave that for another day. I'm think your teacher is ready to start school." He glanced at Eva, and she nodded.

"Nice work. Next time our cattle get out, I'll know who to send for," Michael said and walked away with a woman holding a baby.

Tully coiled the rope again and handed it back to Danny. "I hope I was able to lay your doubts to rest."

"You did that and more. I'm sorry I put you on the spot. Annabeth likes to share the stories you've told her. You appear larger-than-life in them. I'm ashamed to say I was hoping to show her you aren't."

"Don't put too much stock in the stories the kid repeats. One thing you'll find is true about most cowboys. Telling stories is a lot like our boots—they look fine the way they are, but putting some polish on them sure makes 'em shine."

"Did you truly rope a wild coyote?"

"I did, and it was a dumb thing to do. Getting a lasso on an angry coyote is a whole lot easier than getting it off one."

Danny chuckled. "I'll remember that. How long will you be staying with the Beachy family?"

"Until Gideon is up and around, or until Becca stops feeding me. Whichever comes first. She is a fine cook."

"Your help is deeply appreciated," Danny said, looking toward Becca, who was getting in her buggy.

"They are *goot* people," Tully said, following Danny's gaze.

Danny turned to Tully. "I think you are *goot* people, too."

"Me? I don't know about that. If I am it's because Becca makes a fellow want to live up to her expectations."

"She does. I didn't think I would like you, *Englisch*, but I have been wrong before."

"It takes a big man to admit it. It appears Becca is ready to go. It was a pleasure talking to you."

"Likewise, partner," Danny drawled in a poor attempt at a Western accent.

Tully grinned as he walked away and got in the buggy with Becca. He settled back and looked at her. "What did you think of my show?"

She backed the horse away from the hitching rail and turned him around. "It was interesting. What were you and Danny talking about so intently?"

"You," he teased, hoping to see her smile.

Becca scowled at Tully. He had no business discussing her with Danny. "What is that supposed to mean?"

He held up both hands. "Sorry, I was kidding. We agreed you and Gideon are good people and that you are a fine cook. I mean, a so-so, plain cook. I keep forgetting that flattery is not your way."

"Oh." That served her right, assuming she was the main topic of conversation between the two men.

Tully flexed his fingers. "I couldn't believe I could still do some of those tricks. I haven't had a lasso in my hands in years."

"How did you learn such things?" Although it was considered rude to ask about a person's past, she couldn't contain her curiosity about him.

"There was a ranch hand who worked for my grandfather named Carl Littlehorse. Carl had been on the rodeo circuit as a trick roper. He was far better than I could ever hope to be. He used to perform while standing on the back of his horse. He taught me the basics and some tricks. The rest I picked up on my own. A kid has to do something for entertainment."

"Weren't there other children to play with? You must have had schoolmates?"

"We lived a long way from other families. My grand-parents didn't mix much. I had a pair of cousins who lived on the ranch when I was in grade school. They were a few years older than me. My uncle and my grandfather didn't see eye to eye. When my uncle and his family left the ranch, I was pretty much on my own." He turned to stare out the window beside him. "I was always something of a loner, anyway."

Not by choice, she thought. His mother left him, his uncle and cousins left, his grandparents died. It was no wonder Tully reminded her of a lonely little boy who made jokes instead of letting others see his pain.

"Is it difficult to learn roping? I saw Otto do it, so it can't be too hard."

"Some people have a knack for it."

"Could you teach me how to spin a lasso?"

He turned to her with a look of surprise on his face. "Would that be permitted?"

"We are allowed to do some things just for fun."

"Name one besides checkers."

"Horseshoes. Volleyball. Singing. Visiting. At Christmas we go caroling. We have cookie exchange parties. We will even go to the Christmas parade in Presque Isle. In the summer we have picnics and attend the county fair. We women hold quilting bees."

He drew back in mock amazement. "Quilting bees, I do declare. I had no idea the Amish were such a frivolous bunch."

Becca cast him a sidelong glance. "Are you making fun of me?"

"Yes."

She giggled. "I thought so."

"Do you mind?"

She had trouble keeping a smile off her face. "If I say I do, will you stop?"

"No. It's too much fun to tease you."

"Are you ever serious?"

He looked away again. "There have been times in my life when I have been extremely serious. Now isn't one of them."

"What made you serious?"

"Getting shot at, for one."

She turned her startled gaze on him. "Someone was shooting at you? Why?"

"I was a soldier in a place where folks thought a bullet or a bomb was the best way to get rid of me and my buddies. Some of us didn't make it out alive. I saw friends die. I often wonder why I was spared."

Horrified, she struggled to find the right thing to say. "I'm sorry you lost friends."

"Thanks. They were good men and women. So any day I'm not being shot at is a good day for me."

He was trying to turn aside his grief with another joke, but she didn't find it funny. Tully's life had been filled with sadness. She prayed he would know joy from now on. How could she help? There had to be some way to show him life was good and that God meant for His children to enjoy their time on earth. Even if they suffered sorrows as Tully had and as she had, there was still goodness in life. She prayed He would show her the answer.

Tully stared out the window with his lips pressed tightly together. He could've cheerfully bitten his tongue. What was the matter with him? He never talked about losing his friends in the war or feeling left out as a child. If he opened his mouth again, he was likely to tell Becca that he was an alcoholic struggling to stay sober. Like she needed to know that about him. If only she wasn't so sympathetic and easy to talk to, he might have been able to stay silent. She had a way about her that made him want to open up.

In spite of being angry with himself, he realized he didn't mind sharing the unhappy bits of his life with Becca. She had seen her own share of sorrow. She had coped with the sadness in her life much better than he had handled the bad times in his. He turned his head to study her. Maybe it was her faith that gave her such strength. Or perhaps she was simply a strong woman because of the way she had been raised. He had never met anyone quite like her. It was a shame he couldn't take her to a movie or to dinner. She probably wouldn't go out with him even if she wasn't Amish. She was much too smart to fall for a guy like him.

He had never given much thought to starting a family. Becca and Annabeth made him realize how much he was missing out on. If he couldn't ask her out on a date, he might as well entertain her in another fashion.

"I will teach you how to spin a rope if you really want to learn."

"I do. It looks like fun."

If he could bring a little fun into her life with his cowboy antics, then he could prove to be useful after all. "First question. Do you have a rope?"

"Of course we do. We have horses and cows that sometimes need to be restrained. We use a rope for pulling any number of things."

"Okay, that was a silly question. When would you like to start?"

"Tomorrow. It is Saturday. I won't have to take Annabeth to school, so I can make some free time in the morning."

"Okeydoke. It's a date," he said wishing it could be more than a simple lesson. "In exchange I'd like you to teach me to drive a horse. I've ridden a lot of miles on horseback, but we never used driving horses or teams on our ranch. Grandpa owned tractors. I've always wanted to learn."

She held the lines where he could take them. "We don't have to wait until tomorrow for this."

He took the leather straps in his hands. "You trust me enough to give me the reins?"

"I do, but they are called lines. Reins are on the bridle of a riding horse." She scooted closer to show him how to hold them. His heart kicked up a notch at her nearness, but he forced himself to concentrate on what she was saying.

"To make Cider go, you say his name and then 'step walk' or 'step trot.' To make him stop, you say 'whoa,' or you can pull back on the lines. Our corner is just ahead. You might want to slow him down before you try to make the turn."

Tully pulled back, and the horse responded. "Is there a command for turning?"

"'Gee' and 'haw' for left or right. Make sure you say his name first. Use the lines to keep him moving straight on the roadway. He likes to drift out into the center."

"Don't you use Amish words?"

"Most of our horses are already trained by the *En-*

glisch when we buy them. Many of them are former racehorses. There's no point in teaching a horse Amish words because you might want to sell him or her back to the *Englisch* someday. Always say 'good boy' when he does the right thing."

Tully suspected Cider would've turned into his own drive without any prompting, but he dutifully spoke the commands. They didn't end up in the ditch, but he came close enough to make Becca draw a quick breath.

When he drew Cider to a stop in front of the barn, Becca smiled at him. "Not bad."

"Not good."

"We shall see how I do with my first roping lesson tomorrow."

He got out and helped her down, happy for the excuse to hold her hand. He allowed his grip to linger a little longer than was necessary. She didn't pull away.

They stood together silently for long moment with the snow falling gently around them. She kept her gaze down. Her face was partially obscured by the large black bonnet she wore. He wished they weren't wearing gloves. He wanted the warmth of her touch. He longed to cup her chin and lift her face so that she was looking at him. So that he could press his lips to hers.

She squeezed his fingers gently. How could he make time stand still?

He couldn't, and he had no right to think about kissing her. She wasn't a woman he could kiss and walk away from. He knew that in the depths of his soul. And just as surely he knew that he would have to walk away. He didn't belong in her little slice of paradise. He wanted her to remember him fondly, not as a pushy outsider who thought her kindness was an invitation to trifle with her affections.

She looked up at him. He made himself let go of her hand. The loss brought a physical ache in his chest. "I'll put Cider up. You go in and get warm."

He turned away before he could take her in his arms and prove just how weak a man he really was.

"Tully."

He stopped at the sound of her voice but didn't look back. "What?"

"Thank you for telling me about your family and your friends. I understand how difficult it is to talk about loss. I am honored that you shared your feelings with me."

"The thing you need to remember about cowboys is that we like to spin tall tales."

"I think this cowboy doesn't want people to know he carries sadness and guilt in his heart. He covers up what he feels with jokes. Our burdens never truly leave us, but they are made lighter when we share them with someone who cares. I care, Tully. Never forget that. I count you as a dear friend."

He couldn't think of anything funny to say. He swallowed hard against the lump in his throat and led Cider toward the barn.

Chapter Ten

The snow turned into a driving blizzard, and by morning the world outside was a swirling curtain of white. Becca was thankful she didn't have to drive Annabeth to school, but the inclement weather meant her roping lesson would have to wait for a better day. When Tully came into the kitchen, he joined her at the window. "I didn't see this in the forecast," he said.

They depended on the daily newspaper and reports from their *Englisch* neighbors if bad weather was expected. "I don't think it was supposed to get this bad."

"What's with all the clothesline?" He nodded to the five-gallon bucket of it sitting on the counter with the blue line coiled almost to the top inside. Her mind had been so full of thoughts about Tully, worry about Gideon and all that was going on that she had neglected an important task. During a blizzard was not the time to carry it out, but now she had no choice.

"When Bishop Schultz and my grandfather came to welcome us to the community, they brought along a hundred and fifty yards of clothesline and told us how to use it. I should have put it out before now."

"You aren't going to hang out the wash today?"

She bit her lip as she looked at him. "It is so we can find our way to the barn and back in weather like this. In my defense, I spent last winter in Florida. I wasn't expecting winter to come on so soon. I should have had it out before now."

"Oh, I get you. We need to rig up a safety line. Okay, I guess I'll get my coat on."

She shook her head. "I am more familiar with the farm, and this is my fault."

He picked up the bucket. "Stay here. I'll go. You have people depending on you. If this old cowpoke gets lost in a blizzard, he won't be missed by many."

"Oh, Tully, that isn't true." She couldn't bear the thought of him putting himself in danger.

"It's mostly true, so end of discussion. I'll need something to cover my head and my mouth. I don't want my hat to end up in Canada."

Becca gave in. "I have stocking caps and wool scarves here."

She opened a drawer and pulled out several. He took a hunter-orange hat and a thick, wide black scarf. He put the hat on, wrapped the scarf over his face, then slipped into Gideon's heavy overcoat and gloves.

She handed him the bucket and put on her own coat and bonnet. "*Gott* will protect you. The line has knots in it every ten yards. If you go past ten of them, you have missed the barn. I will give you three jerks on the line so you will know to walk to your left and then to the right until you find the fence or the building. Whatever you do, Tully, don't let go of the rope."

"Not a chance. Me and ropes are old friends." He tied a small loop in the end and slipped it over his arm so he couldn't drop it. "See?"

"All right." Becca stepped out onto the porch with Tully beside her. They made a pass around the porch post, and Becca got ready to feed the line out of the bucket. "Be careful." She shouted to be heard over the wind.

"This is not a day for funny stuff," he said and stepped out into the blizzard.

He was gone from sight within ten feet of the house. Her heart rose in her throat. He was risking his life for her and her family's safety. Did he realize that?

Keep him safe, Lord.

She played out the line as he walked, making sure it was still taut. He would be okay. She knew it. She had faith. She could feel jerks along the sturdy rope as he moved farther away. She thought he was still headed in the right general direction then realized that was because the line went through the front gate. Once he was beyond that point, she had no way of knowing for sure.

She tried to judge how long he had been gone, but time seemed to drag to a standstill. She counted the knots as they came up out of the bucket and squinted to see into the blowing snow. She couldn't even make out the gate, which she knew was only twenty feet in front of her. When the tenth knot slipped through her gloves, she knew he had missed the barn. She gripped the line and tugged on it three times. He tugged back the same number. Was he left or right of the building?

He was in God's hands, but she couldn't stop the worry that wiggled into her mind. Then the line went slack. What was wrong? Had he lost his hold on it? He would be blind without it. The urge to go out and search until she found him was overwhelming. Only the knowledge that she could be pulling the line farther out of his reach kept her from jerking on it again. Even if she reached the end of the rope, she could bypass by him without knowing it.

Keep him safe, Lord. Bring him back to me.

Just when she thought she couldn't bear it another moment, the line went tight again, and her knees sagged with relief. She held on to it, relishing the tiny movements that meant he was moving. Three hard jerks on the line signaled he was on his way back. When he loomed out of the snow, she grabbed hold of him, pulled him up the steps and into the kitchen. His stocking hat and scarf were crusted with snow, as were his eyelashes. She shook him. "I told you not to let go of the line. What happened?"

He blinked hard as he stared at her. "I didn't let go."

"But the line went slack. I almost headed out to find you."

"I missed the barn, but then I found the corral. I must've let the line sag when I followed the fence to the corner of the barn. Then I tied it off and followed it back. Some of the drifts I struggled through were three feet deep. I couldn't see my hand in front of my face."

She kept her tight grip on his arm as her panic-induced anger faded and her wildly beating heart calmed down. "You gave me a terrible fright. I don't know what I would have done if anything had happened to you."

He patted her hand and pulled the scarf away from his face to reveal his adorable grin. "I'm sorry I scared you, but I'm fine. What's for breakfast?"

She shook her head. "You and your stomach. We have to milk first, but we won't take it to the collection station until this blows over. It will freeze, but that can't be helped. We can still sell it."

"I hope the Fisher brothers don't try to get here in this."

"They are not foolish men. They know we can manage, even if it will take us longer without them."

His expression changed as he stared at her. "Were you truly concerned about me?"

She laid a hand on his cold cheek. "Of course I was. You could have easily been lost."

His gaze softened. "I'm not worth the worry, Becca."

She wanted to move away, but his eyes held her captive. What was he thinking? She longed to ask him. She wanted to know everything about him. Why did he value himself so poorly? She pulled her hand away. "You are worth far more than you think. That was a brave thing you did."

His eyes darkened. The ice on his lashes began melting and ran down his face like tears. He rubbed them away and walked to the sink, where she had four of the milk pails waiting. He leaned on the counter with both arms and bowed his head. "If I had known how hard this was going to be, I don't think I would've stayed."

She knew he wasn't talking about the work. The last thing she wanted was to heap more sorrow on him. Yet that was exactly what she was doing. She was woman enough to know that Tully was attracted to her. While she faced her own growing affection for him, there couldn't be anything but friendship between them. All else was forbidden. "Tully, I'm sorry—"

"I get it," he said, cutting off her explanation. "The cows are waiting." He turned to face her, holding out the pails. She gathered her scattered wits and took two of the buckets from him and then followed him out the door.

* * *

Tully had never been in this position before. Attracted to a woman who was so far out of his reach that he would've been better off trying to pluck the stars out of the sky. A beautiful, kind, caring woman who was not for the likes of him, a man who'd made a wreck of his life. She still mourned her husband.

Telling himself that she couldn't possibly find him attractive wasn't doing the trick. Because when she looked at him with such kindness in her eyes, he could almost imagine it was affection. He'd thought he was done deluding himself when he checked into rehab. He'd had to accept the harsh reality of his addiction. Now he had to face the fact that he was falling hard for a woman who deserved a much better man. He needed to keep those feelings in check.

He followed behind her on the guideline. Twice he had to help her back to her feet when she stumbled in the deep snow and fell. He would need to shovel a path to the barn when the snow stopped blowing so walking wasn't so treacherous. How deep would the snow be by the end of the winter? He hated to think of Gideon out shoveling this even after his injury was healed.

When they reached the barn and stepped inside, it was wonderfully peaceful compared to the storm raging outside. He drew a deep breath, inhaling the smells of old wood, fresh hay and animals. The cows mooed at the sight of them, happy to have their humans arrive to milk and feed them. He stopped to pat Diamond as she poked her head between the slats of the gate. She was getting cuter by the day, with long eyelashes framing her huge dark eyes on either side of her white patch.

Becca walked past him to start milking on the farthest cow. She didn't say anything.

He leaned down to Diamond. "I have to learn to keep my mouth shut. Every time I speak to her, I end up saying something I shouldn't."

He and Becca finished milking in awkward silence.

Gideon and Annabeth were in the kitchen when Tully and Becca came in. If the old man was in much pain, it didn't show. He smiled at Tully. "How are my cows?"

"No signs of illness or infection. The blizzard is making them nervous. They didn't give quite as much milk, but everyone was eating when we put out the silage."

"Can I go see Diamond after breakfast?" Annabeth asked.

"No," Tully and Becca said together. "It's snowing too hard," Becca added. "We will all stay in today."

"Are you coming to church with us tomorrow?" Annabeth asked Tully.

"I hadn't thought about it. I guess tomorrow is Sunday." He glanced toward Becca, who was busy at the stove. Going to church with her seemed preferable to staying home by himself. "If the weather improves, maybe I'll ride along with you folks."

"I advise against it," Gideon said abruptly, surprising Tully.

"Why?" Annabeth looked puzzled. Tully wondered the same thing.

"Tully will not understand the preaching or the singing. He will feel out of place. There is an *Englisch* church not far from Michael Shetler's home in New Covenant where our service is being held tomorrow.

If you wish to worship, you will be more comfortable there. I'm told Pastor Frank Pearson is a fine preacher."

Tully hadn't been inside a church in a long time, but he suspected Becca would think better of him if he made the effort to go. He wanted her approval. "I can do that."

"I still think Tully would like to come with us." Annabeth glanced at her grandfather with a small pout to her lips.

"Tully is welcome to join us for the meal after the service," Becca said softly with a pointed glance in his direction.

Gideon nodded. "That would be acceptable."

"Sounds fine to me," Tully said. His heart grew lighter at the sight of her little smile. He wanted things to go back to the way they had been between them. Friendly.

Annabeth beamed. "Then he can show us more rope tricks."

"No, sweetheart, I'm done with rope tricks," he said. "Once was enough. I don't want folks to think I'm a show-off."

Her expression fell, but she nodded. "We must be humble and not put ourselves above others. Everyone is equal in the eyes of *Gott*." She looked to her grandfather, who nodded in approval.

"How is the rehearsal for your Christmas play going?" Gideon asked.

"Jenny wants her new nephew to be the baby Jesus, but Teacher doesn't think we should have a real baby in the play." Annabeth rolled her eyes. "She's afraid he'll cry through the whole thing. I told her babies cry sometimes. No one will care."

Tully caught Becca's eyes and struggled not to laugh. She carried a platter of French toast and sausages to the table and sat down. "Since she is getting married and giving up her position, your teacher wants her first and only Christmas play to be a success. I think using a doll would be better than having everyone shout their lines over the noise of a crying *bobbli*."

Their times together at the table had become one of the things he liked best about this family. It was how he always thought family time should be. There wasn't a lot of idle chatter. Plans for the day were made, duties laid out, but there was an underlying connection between Becca, Annabeth and Gideon that didn't need words. It was a bond he wished he could share.

They all bowed their heads to say a silent blessing. He would ask Gideon later what he said when he prayed. Tully wanted to be able to pray as they did.

After breakfast he went to his room. He took out his phone, sat on the edge of his bed and dialed Arnie's number. His buddy picked up on the fifth ring. "Cowboy, do you have any idea what time it is?"

"It's morning."

"It's Saturday morning, and it isn't even eight o'clock yet."

Tully pulled the phone away from his ear to look at the display. It read 7:55. "Sorry, I've been up for hours. Do you want me to call back later?"

"No, I'm awake now. Where are you?"

"I'm still on an Amish dairy farm near a place called New Covenant."

"You made it a whole week. I didn't think you would last two days. How do you survive without electricity?"

"I go to bed when it gets dark or I light a lamp." He

didn't bother to explain that he still reached for a light switch every time he entered a room. Some habits were hard to break.

"How are you keeping your phone charged?"

"I have a car charger."

"Are you still sober?"

"I'm happy to say that I am. It feels good."

"I'm proud of you, man. How is the pretty Amish widow?"

Tully couldn't think of a way to answer that.

"Did we get cut off?" Arnie asked.

"I'm still here. Her name is Becca Beachy. She is an amazing woman."

"Wow. That didn't take long. She must be something special if she caught your eye."

"Something special doesn't begin to describe her." She was everything good and kind. A wonderful mother and so much more.

"How does she feel about you?" Arnie asked.

Tully rubbed the palm of his free hand on his thigh. "She considers me a friend. A dear friend."

"That sounds promising. Have you asked her out?"

"I've thought about it, but what would be the point? Friendship or matrimony are the only two options a woman like her would accept. I'm not husband material. You know that as well as I do, so I don't see any point in pursuing a relationship."

"That's a bunch of malarkey. I'm not saying you should marry someone you just met. In fact I'm saying *don't* marry someone you've only known a week, but you will make a great husband when the time comes. You have a lot of heart, Tully. I hate to see you letting it go to waste."

"Thanks, but don't flatter me. That is not the Amish way. Becca needs a friend, not a suitor. I'll be content being her friend, although she deserves better."

"If you think you're not good enough for this woman…then become the kind of friend she deserves."

"What do you mean?"

"Exactly what I said. The first thing you need is to believe in yourself. You're the best of all possible friends. You'd do anything for her and her family. You fake it until you make it."

"If only it was that easy."

"I'm sorry if I sound flippant, Tully. It's too early to dispense advice to the lovelorn. So other than a crush on Becca, how is it living in the Stone Age?"

"Don't make fun of them. You don't know what these people are like. They are genuinely happy living the simplest of lives. Did you know they only go to school until the eighth grade?"

"What I know about the Amish you couldn't spread on a cracker. What I know about you, on the other hand, is that you don't believe you deserve happiness. You need to work on your self-esteem."

"I wouldn't know where to start."

"The Amish are religious, so start going to church. I hear all good things about the experience. Not that I go much myself. Start looking for a job so when the old geezer is back on his feet you'll have something lined up. I know there are a lot of farms down that way. You should fit right in. What did she say when you told her that you are an alcoholic in recovery?"

"It hasn't come up." Tully braced for his friend's explosion.

Arnie sighed heavily. "You've only known her a

week, so I'm going to let that slide, but if you want to become the kind of friend she deserves, then you need to be honest with her."

"Thanks, Arnie. I'll let you get back to sleep."

"Okay. You'll still be here for Christmas, won't you?"

"I'm staying to see Annabeth's school program on Christmas Eve, but I'll be at your place Christmas morning. That's the plan."

"Good. See you then."

Tully hung up, but Arnie's advice still rang in his ears. *Become the kind of friend she deserves.* He had stayed because he wanted to be the hero of the moment for Becca and her family. It hadn't quite turned out that way. How could he open up about his biggest failure and his biggest regret—that his addiction had led to the death of his closest friend and others?

Arnie was wrong. Tully didn't need to share that part of who he was with Becca. He would be leaving in a few weeks. He wanted her to remember him as the cowboy who rode in to save the day. Even if he hadn't.

Chapter Eleven

The storm blew itself out during the evening. By morning there wasn't a cloud in the sky to obscure the stars that were still out when Becca and Tully went to the barn. A half-moon hanging above the horizon left the snow-covered landscape almost as bright as day. He tramped a path through the snow that was thigh-deep in places and helped her along. Tully was careful to keep the conversation casual. If she noticed he was quieter than usual, she didn't comment on it.

The sun was just rising when they finished. Tully followed Becca along the narrow path toward the house. He stopped and cocked his head to the side. Did he hear sleigh bells?

The sound grew louder. He looked toward the lane and saw four magnificent high-stepping Belgian draft horses hitched abreast come charging into sight. Snow flew up from their hooves. Their breath made clouds of white around their heads as the sun glinted off their shiny caramel-colored backs and brass harness bells. An Amish man he didn't know stood on a wedge-shaped road grader behind them, a mountain of a man who looked as if he could handle the massive team easily.

He pulled to a stop in front of the house. The horses tossed their heads and snorted, seeming eager to be off again. "*Guder mariye*, Becca," he called out. "You shouldn't have any trouble getting to church service now. You are the last home on my route."

"*Danki*, Jesse. I was wondering if we would have to take the sleigh."

"My boys can break through most any drift as long as it's not higher than their heads." He nodded to her and spoke softly to his team. They lunged into their collars, pulling the grader easily and leaving a cleared path nearly ten feet wide with snow piled high on either side behind them.

"That man gives new meaning to the word *horsepower*." Tully watched in amazement as they made one more pass around the yard and went out the lane.

Becca chuckled. "Jesse Crump has a fine team. He and his wife farm on the other side of New Covenant, and he works for the bishop building garden sheds."

"How much does it cost to have your driveway plowed by four giant horses?"

She looked perplexed. "There is no charge. Jesse does it because it is needed."

"For everyone in your Amish community?" How many hours had the man been up clearing roads?

"And for some of our *Englisch* neighbors. We take care of each other."

She went into the house. He followed her after one last glance at the open lane. Tully could still hear the jingle of harness bells in the distance. "The mountain man gives new meaning to the word *neighborly*, too," he muttered to himself. He found more to admire about the Amish every day he was among them.

The next half hour was a flurry of activity as everyone got ready for church. Tully cleaned and shined his boots and put on his best pair of jeans along with a blue-and-white-striped Western shirt adorned with pearl snaps.

When he came into the kitchen, he saw Gideon dressed in a black suit with a vest. Becca wore a dark blue dress with a snow-white apron and a freshly starched *kapp* on her head. Annabeth sat in a chair while her mother fixed her hair. Tully watched in amazement as she combed, folded and pinned Annabeth's thick auburn tresses into a type of flat bun on the back of her head. Becca settled her daughter's *kapp* over the bun and pinned it into place.

"That's amazing."

"What is?" Becca asked, adding a bobby pin to her own *kapp*.

"That you can get so much hair under those things."

"It's easy." She turned around. Her mouth dropped open in surprise.

He looked down at his shirt and jeans. "Is something wrong?"

Annabeth gave a big nod. "You are not plain enough, Tully. But your buttons are very pretty."

"They're snaps." He demonstrated by popping them open and closed on his cuff. He looked from Becca to Gideon, who were both still staring at him.

Gideon cleared his throat. "You look *goot* for an *Englischer*."

"But much too fancy to be an Amish fellow," Annabeth added.

Becca had recovered her composure. "You look okay. Are we ready?" She collected a large box from the table and headed for the door. Tully jumped to open it for her. Annabeth followed her mother. Gideon came slowly on his crutches with his injured leg held stiffly out in front of him. Tully grabbed his jean jacket and stayed close behind the old man until he was safely settled in the front seat of the buggy.

"I'm going to follow you in my car."

Becca nodded. "All right."

The trip to New Covenant took about twenty-five minutes on the snowy road. He stayed behind them with his amber lights flashing to warn people coming up behind him that there was a slow-moving vehicle ahead. Almost everybody slowed down. Only two cars shot around them. One was a red sports car whose driver felt it was necessary to blast his horn in the process.

They passed Annabeth's school and turned into a farm not far beyond it. There were already a dozen buggies lined up beside the barn. He recognized Michael Shetler leading a horse, still wearing his harness, away from one of the buggies toward the open barn door. Otto met him and took the horse inside.

Michael came to Tully's car door. Tully rolled down the window. "Have you come to worship with us?" Michael asked.

"Gideon didn't think it would be a good idea. He suggested I go to an English church not far from here. Can you give me directions?"

"To Pastor Frank's church? Sure. Go back out on the highway and go left to the first intersection. Follow the road toward Fort Craig. You will see the church on the left side of the road just after you get into town. Tell Frank I'll be late for our regular meeting this week."

"I'll do that. Becca said I should come back for the meal. About what time would that be?"

"Our meetings last about three and a half hours, so if you return close to noon, there should be something left for you to eat."

"Thanks a lot." Tully watched Becca help Gideon out of their buggy. He started to get out of the car to assist her but quickly saw she had more than enough help as numerous men, including the mountainous Jesse, came to her aid. She glanced his way and lifted her hand in a small wave. He did the same. A moment later she was surrounded by a group of women, and they all went inside the house.

A familiar sense of loneliness took hold of him, although he tried to ignore it. Becca and Gideon had made him feel so much at home that seeing them surrounded by other Amish while he sat in a car made him aware of just how far apart they truly were. He put the car in gear and followed Michael's directions.

Near the outskirts of the town, a small building caught his eye. The sign above it said Lumberjack Bar. The parking lot was empty, but that wasn't unusual for any bar at this time of day. He drove on, glad he didn't have to face that temptation when he was already feeling ill at ease.

Finally he saw the small white church he'd been told about. He turned into the paved parking lot that had been cleared of snow. A beat-up orange truck with a snowplow on the front was parked at the far end of the lot. It might do the trick, but it sure wasn't as pretty as Jesse's big horses.

Tully got out of his car. Either he was among the first to arrive, or Pastor Frank had a really small congregation. He met the preacher just inside the door. The middle-aged man dressed in black looked Tully up and down. "An unfamiliar face. Welcome to the Lord's Community Church. Are you here to attend worship, or do you need directions to somewhere else?"

"I've been told that you're a good preacher. I thought I should come see for myself."

"Then you are doubly welcome. Would you happen to be the cowboy that's staying with Gideon Beachy and his family?"

His question took Tully aback. "How could you know that?"

"The Amish children around here used to attend our public school. Many have remained friends with their former classmates. The story of your ability with a rope spread quickly, including to my next-door neighbor's children, who hurried over to tell me about it."

"For people who don't use telephones, the Amish don't have trouble spreading news."

Pastor Frank chuckled. "That is the truth." He glanced at his watch. "It's almost time to begin. Please find a seat."

"Before I forget, Michael Shetler said he would be late to his regular meeting with you."

"Thank you for the reminder. I have had a change of plans. I'll have to let Michael know."

"I can give him the message."

"Great. The new days and times for our meetings are in the bulletin." He took one from the bookshelf behind him and gave it to Tully.

There were more people coming in now. Tully moved

to a pew at the back. While he waited for the service to begin, he scanned the paper Pastor Frank had given him. He saw the note about time changes for several meetings. One in particular caught his attention. The regular AA meeting had been moved from Friday to Saturday evening at six. The other meetings were for bereavement and survivors. He wondered which one of the three Michael attended.

Tully rolled up the paper. It was good to know there was an AA meeting available to him if he needed it while he was staying with the Beachys. Would he be able to remain anonymous in such a small, tight-knit community, or would word of his addiction get back to Becca before he got home from the meeting? It made him hesitate to attend. So far he hadn't needed the support the way he had when he was back in the city, but that was only because he fell into bed every night too tired to even think about driving out to find a drink.

He took note of the well-dressed families around him. A few members wore jeans with nice shirts or sweaters, although none wore the Western style he favored. He gathered more than a few inquisitive glances, making him feel like an outsider in a group where everyone knew each other. Several young children moved along the pews, climbing over their parents and fussing. Some of the teenagers looked bored. They checked their phones frequently. Older people sat quietly with their heads bowed.

A woman with a pink streak in her blond hair began playing the organ up front. Around him folks lifted their hymnals and flipped through the pages. What the congregation lacked in harmonious voices they made up for with their enthusiasm. Tully didn't bother trying to sing. He could twirl a rope, but when he tried to sing in a group like this, he sounded like a frog with a sore throat. Singing to the cows was a different story. They didn't care what he sounded like, so he was able to carry half a tune.

Pastor Frank turned out to be an interesting speaker. Tully heard his message of a child's anticipation for the arrival of Christmas and hoped-for presents under the tree. The pastor used it to show the world's anticipation for the arrival of God's only son on earth. Tully believed in God—he just wasn't sure God believed in or cared about him.

He didn't stick around after the service was over. It had only been little more than an hour, but he was already missing Becca.

He drove back to Michael Shetler's place, intending to sit in his car until the Amish service was over. The sound of singing reached him when he shut off the engine. He rolled down his window.

The song wasn't like the hymns at Pastor Frank's church. There wasn't any music, just voices raised together in slow, almost mournful undulation. They were singing in German—he recognized some of the lyrics. He got out of his car and moved onto the porch to hear better. The front door opened. A small boy of about three or four darted out quickly, followed by an older boy, who scooped him up. As they turned back, Tully recognized the kid as one from Annabeth's school.

The boy grinned. "Hello, Cowboy. Do you have your rope handy? My little *brudder* is having trouble sitting still this morning."

"Sorry, I don't."

"I'm joking. Come in."

"Are you sure it's okay?"

The boy nodded and went in, carrying his brother. Tully followed slowly. Inside he saw benches set up in rows with a narrow center aisle. The women sat on one side. Men sat on the other. He saw Gideon sitting near the front on a kitchen chair with his leg propped up with a pillow on a low stool. Tully quickly picked out Becca across the room with Annabeth beside her, and something in his chest eased. Simply seeing her made him feel better, happier.

The man preaching in Amish at the front of the room paid no attention to Tully. Off to his side Tully saw the younger boys occupied the last row of benches. Otto sat on the end beside the boy with the runaway toddler. Otto scooted over and patted the bench beside him. Tully smiled his thanks and sat down.

"Do you want me to tell you what the preacher is saying?" Otto asked in a low whisper.

"If it's okay, sure."

For the next hour, Tully listened to Otto relay what the minister and then the bishop spoke about. Some of it he was able to gather for himself when the bishop read from the German Bible he held. It was Matthew, chapter one. The messages preached were about remaining humble and keeping the true meaning of Christmas in hearts and minds during the season. The bishop asked his congregation not to be distracted by the colorful decorations and fancy gifts their *Englisch* neighbors used to celebrate the season but rather to remember it was a babe born in a lowly stable who quietly brought salvation to mankind.

When the next hymn started, Otto handed Tully a large black book and opened it for him. There weren't any musical notes, just the lyrics written in German on one side of the page with the English translation beside it. Tully listened to the worshipers singing and realized Gideon had been wrong. Tully didn't feel uncomfortable. The deep faith of those around him was as warm as if a blanket had been laid about his shoulders.

"Is it strange having an *Englisch* fellow live with you?" Becca's friend Gemma Crump asked as they set out food on the tables following the preaching.

"It was a little strange at first, but I'm getting used to Tully. He certainly keeps Gideon from fussing." His presence also decreased her loneliness, but she didn't share that with her friends.

Gemma glanced at Becca from under lowered brows. "What does Danny think about the arrangement?"

"I'm not aware of how Danny feels about Tully, and I'm not sure I'd care. He did voice some concerns about Tully's influence on Annabeth, but other than her fascination with his storytelling and rope tricks, I don't see that she is being harmed by knowing him." Annabeth was playing outside with her friends.

"I wish I could've seen his demonstration with his lasso," Gemma's mother, Dinah, said, setting out coffee cups.

"I saw it," Bethany, Michael's wife, said. "It was impressive."

It had also been a glaring reminder that he wasn't one of them. As had been the clothes he had on that morning. She had only seen him wearing his chambray shirts and dark jeans. They weren't so very different from the clothing worn by other young men in the community, except Tully wore a belt with a large buckle. Amish men only wore suspenders.

"He sat in on the last of our service," Dinah said looking out the window.

"I saw him." Becca tried to sound as if it didn't matter, but her heart had given a happy little leap knowing he was near again. It was amazing and frightening to know how much she had come to want his presence.

"I overheard Gideon telling Leroy that Tully has a wonderful sense of humor," Dinah said. "My Leroy only thinks he is funny," she added with a wry smile.

Gemma giggled. "I may tell *Daed* you said that."

Becca looked at her friends. Should she say anything? She was troubled by the unhappiness Tully tried to hide with his jokes and stories. She focused on cutting the apple pies she had in front of her. "He tells wonderful tales, but he uses humor to hide his pain. From what I have gathered, his life has been filled with sorrow and unhappy memories. I want to change that."

When no one said anything, Becca looked up. They were staring at her with shocked expressions on their faces. "What?"

"It sounds as though you have come to care for this young man," Dinah said.

"As a friend," Becca said quickly. The younger women looked relieved, but Dinah retained her look of concern.

"He feels bad about injuring our calf." Becca tried to explain what she wanted. "I'm sure that's part of why he offered to stay on and help when Gideon was hurt, but there is more to it. Tully has no family, no home to go to, not even a job to support himself, and yet he spends his time making us laugh and offering his help for nothing except food and a place to sleep. He has said he will stay until after the school program as his gift to Annabeth. I want to give Tully a Christmas season that he will remember fondly when he leaves us. As our gift to him. That's what I mean."

Gemma glanced at the other women in the room. "We give our *Englisch* neighbors candy or breads for them to enjoy. We sing carols to spread the joy of the season. Giving is something we all must practice."

"That's what I would like to do for Tully. I want us to share our gift of a plain Christmas season. I want him to feel included, not simply tolerated. Do you think that's wrong?"

"I don't," Bethany said. "I'm sure we can come up with a dozen ways to make his stay with us special."

Dinah grinned and nodded. "It is charity to a stranger. Are we not instructed by the words of Jesus to be good Samaritans? The bishop has met Tully and agreed that it was acceptable for him to stay with you. I think he will like this idea of including Tully in our celebrations."

The outside door opened, and Bishop Schultz, along with Leroy Lapp and Tully, came in together. The bishop and Leroy were laughing heartily. "That's a fine story, Tully," Leroy said.

The bishop slapped Tully's back. "I will share it in the Christmas cards to my brothers and sisters who live in Ohio. A rooster riding a pig all the way through Arthurville. I would've liked to see that."

The bishop sobered when he realized the women were staring at him. "Shall I call the community into eat?"

"We are ready," Dinah said with a smile. She leaned

closer to Becca. "I have a feeling this is going to be a wonderful Christmas season."

Becca smiled at Tully. "I couldn't agree more."

The men went through the line first and took their places at the backless benches that had been stacked to make tables. Tully came at the end of the line. Becca added a large piece of cherry pie to a plate that was already loaded with thick slices of bread, cold cuts, cheese spreads and pickled beets. He smiled at her. "You looked like the cat that swallowed the canary when I walked in. What gives?"

"My friends and I were simply making plans for the Christmas season."

"And?"

"And nothing else. Go sit and eat. There are others waiting for a place at the tables."

"I thought I might sit with you."

"Oh *nee*," Dinah said at Becca's elbow. "Men and women eat at separate tables, just as we sit on opposite sides during our worship."

"That would explain why the young people outside don't seem to be in a hurry to eat."

"They know there is plenty, and their turn will come after the older members are finished," Dinah said.

"And in the meantime, the boys and the girls can visit and make eyes at each other," Tully added.

Dinah frowned. "Who is making eyes at what girl?"

"The tall girl with glasses is making eyes at Moses Fisher," he said.

"My niece?" Dinah squeaked and moved to the window to look out.

Becca exchanged a glance with Gemma and smothered a laugh. Tully crossed the room and sat at a table where he could see her. While he wasn't exactly making eyes at her, she soon grew uncomfortable under his scrutiny. She left her serving table and went around to fill coffee cups.

"Please stop staring at me," she said softly as she handed him a cup of piping-hot liquid. She hissed as some of it splashed on her fingers when she set it down.

"Then don't stand in my line of vision. Why are all the women looking at me and smiling like they know something I don't?"

"Are you done eating?"

"If you're that eager to get rid of me, I am." He pulled a handkerchief from his pocket, dipped it in his glass of water and handed it to her. "Wrap this around your hand."

She looked around to see who might be watching, but no one was looking their way. She took it from him, wound it around her stinging fingers and nodded her thanks before moving on to the next table.

After Tully left the room, Becca was able to concentrate on her tasks. Although she would normally stay and visit with her friends, she went to Gideon to see if he was ready to leave. His cough was much better, but she noticed his leg was swelling above his shoe.

"I'd like to visit longer, but I'm ready to go home. Where is Annabeth?"

"Playing outside. I'll get her. Where is Tully?"

"I heard him say there is a game of horseshoes being thrown in the barn. It's a game he enjoys almost as much as checkers. I'm sure you'll find him there."

Becca walked down to the barn. There was a competition going on, but Tully wasn't one of the players. He was watching the game. When he caught sight of her, he nodded toward the door, got up and left the building. Curious, she followed him outside and saw him walk around the side of the building.

When she turned the corner, he was waiting for her. "Let me see your hand."

She still had his damp handkerchief wrapped around it. "It's fine. Just a little scald."

"Does it hurt?"

"Nee."

"The only burn that doesn't hurt is a third-degree burn, and that is serious. Am I going to have to arm wrestle you to get a look at it?"

She relinquished her hand but turned her face away from him. He gently unwound the bandage and turned her hand over. "It's blistered. Don't tell me it doesn't sting."

"Only a little," she admitted.

"Shall I kiss it and make it better?" he asked softly.

Did he think that's what she wanted? He didn't seem to understand how impossible such a thing was. How could she turn his affections aside without hurting him? "Please don't make fun of me."

"Okay, I'm sorry." He looked contrite as he packed a little snow into the handkerchief and wrapped it around her hand again. He didn't release her fingers. Nor did she pull away.

He sighed softly. "I need you to tell me the truth, Becca."

What was he going to ask? If he wanted to know the reason for her racing pulse, could she say it was because of him? She slipped her hand away from his.

Chapter Twelve

"What are you and your friends up to?"

Tully saw Becca relax and was glad he had defused the moment. He also realized how close he had come to kissing her. Would she have let him? Before he took that step, he would have to tell her about his addiction if there was even a chance of something between them.

She moved back. The troubled look in her eyes vanished, and a small smile appeared. "I have no idea what you're talking about. I have told you we were making Christmas plans and nothing else."

"If you say so." He wasn't convinced.

"Gideon is ready to go home. You are welcome to stay and visit with the people here. Gideon says you enjoy playing horseshoes."

"Another time, maybe. I'll follow you home."

"Don't hurry. We do only necessary work on Sunday."

Annabeth came rushing around the corner of the barn. "There you are. *Daadi* is in the buggy and ready to go. Can I ride home with Tully in his car?"

Becca shook her head. "It is not permitted to ride

to or from our prayer meetings in a car. The horse and buggy are our identity. It is the way we show our adherence to the ways of our forefathers, particularly on a day of worship."

Annabeth looked disappointed but nodded in understanding. Tully took her hand and began walking toward the buggy. "I was about to suggest we all go for a Sunday drive later. I'll change that to another day. You can have a ride in my car soon, I promise."

"Maybe you could take me to school tomorrow?" she asked hopefully.

He glanced at Becca. She didn't appear upset by the idea. "Your mother and I will discuss it just as soon as she tells me what she's planning that she doesn't want me to know about."

Annabeth cocked her head to the side. "What?"

They reached the buggy. "Tully is making a joke," Becca said, giving him a saucy grin. She opened the door and got in.

Tully lifted Annabeth and put her in the back seat. "You find out what she's up to and report back to me."

"There's nothing to tell," Becca said over her shoulder. "Cider, step walk."

Tully stood back as they rolled away. Jesse walked up to him. "I hear you are a horseshoe player. Care for a match?"

Tully looked the big man up and down. "Do you take the shoes off the horse or do you throw all four at once?"

Jesse's face split into a wide grin. "Ha. I throw them all at once. It's not hard. The tough part is training the horse to keep his feet together when he lands on the stake."

Tully laughed. "I don't have a comeback for that. One game, then I have to go."

It was easier said than done. He ended up playing Jesse and being soundly beaten. He was able to best Michael twice but lost to Danny. When the bishop stepped up to play him, Tully wondered if he should let the head of the church win. He didn't need to worry. The bishop whomped him. Tully hadn't enjoyed himself so much in a long time.

When he arrived at Becca's home later, Annabeth met him at the door. "*Mamm* won't tell me what she's planning."

He patted the child's head. "Thanks for trying." He met Becca's eyes across the kitchen and managed a smile. "Annabeth, do you want to hear about the time I jumped out of the barn loft with my grandma's best umbrella for a parachute?"

"Sure. I love your stories, Tully." She reached up and took his hand.

He winked at her. "I love sharing them with you, but your mother can't hear this one unless she tells me what she has planned."

Becca pointed to the other room. "Out of my kitchen, both of you. There's nothing to tell."

He couldn't get Becca to admit she was planning something that evening or again the next morning as they entered the barn.

"I wish you would quit asking me." She scowled at him, and he decided not to annoy the cook.

The Fisher brothers didn't show up to help, so he knew they must have gone to their weddings. Tully was gratified they thought he was enough help for Becca and Gideon and hadn't arranged for anyone else to give him a hand. Becca suggested they let Rosie out into the corral for a while to give her a break from her baby. Tully held the calf while Becca led Mama out. He gave the calf a thorough checking over. She was outgrowing her cast. Her leg still had good circulation, so he knew it could wait another day. The vet would be out to see her tomorrow.

He got busy with the milking and realized how much he was starting to enjoy his time with Gideon's big cows. It was still hard work, but his muscles were adjusting.

He had his head pressed to the flank of Maude as he listened to Becca milking the cow behind him. He was almost keeping up with the splashes of milk into her pail. Working together the way they did gave him a sense of rightness. He had a lot of things he wanted to know about her, but he wasn't sure if she would be offended by his questions. He decided to risk it.

"Becca, can I ask you something?"

"I'm making pancakes for breakfast, if that's what you want to know."

He could hear the smile in her voice even though he couldn't see her. "My stomach appreciates the information, but that's not what I was going to ask. Why haven't you remarried?"

He could tell she had quit milking. After a few long moments of silence, she started up again. "There isn't any single reason why I haven't other than I'm not ready."

"Because of your grief for your husband."

"That is part of it. Another reason is not wanting Annabeth to think of someone else as her father. Perhaps that's selfish of me. Then Gideon has lost so much. I want him to feel that we need him. Perhaps *Gott* has not sent the right person to me yet."

"But if the right person came along, you would consider it?" He was far from the right person, but he knew there was something between them. He just wasn't sure what it was.

"Maybe, but it is hard to imagine. Can I ask you a question, Tully?"

She hadn't given him an outright no. "Sure. Anything."

"Did you enjoy yourself yesterday?"

He didn't even have to think that one over. "I did. I liked meeting Pastor Frank. I appreciate what I could understand of your service. Everyone made me feel welcome. I haven't been to church much recently, but I believe I'll start attending again. You and Gideon have so much faith that I would like to find some of that for myself."

"That's wonderful. I'm so glad for you. The Lord uses us all to His purpose."

Her words were encouraging. "I suppose that's true."

Diamond began bawling in her stall. She was tired of being by herself. He chuckled. "He certainly used an odd way to get me to stop here."

"The calf might have made you stop, but I think it was the desire to serve that *Gott* put in your heart that made you stay. You have brightened what could've been a very difficult time for my family."

"I'm happy to oblige." And he was. Maybe happier than he had been in a long time. He was starting to feel useful and not like a burden. Not since leaving the ranch had he felt like he belonged somewhere the way he was starting to feel that he could belong here.

It was a wild idea. There was no reason to think Becca wanted him, but what if she did? They hadn't known each other very long, but they seemed to fit together. He was afraid to discover if time would prove him right or if this would be one more failed mission.

Becca wondered if this was what the Lord had planned for Tully all along, a happy time with a family who cared about him. He seemed more cheerful today. She had heard all about his horseshoe games last evening, and she was glad she had told Gemma and Bethany to ask their husbands to invite him to play. Some of the women from the community would be coming over on Sunday to bake cookies to take in gift boxes to the local nursing home. They would discuss other activities to include Tully when he was occupied. She nearly giggled at the thought of planning his entertainment practically under his nose. She quickly sobered. He might not appreciate that she had made him a charity case for the community.

She stood up with her full bucket. "This is the last one. Were you serious about driving Annabeth to school?"

"In the car? Sure. Do you think her teacher will mind?"

She knew Eva wouldn't care. "Many of the children went to the public school on a bus before New Covenant opened its own school this year. I don't see that it will be a problem. It's not like we will make a habit of it," she added sternly so he would know Annabeth wasn't to wheedle future rides out of him.

"Okay, I'll take her after breakfast. You did say pancakes, didn't you? And maybe some of those little sausage patties and fried potatoes with onions. How about some of those light fluffy biscuits of yours, if that isn't too much trouble?"

"You will have toast and no complaints. I must get you a pair of suspenders for Christmas, because by then you won't be able to buckle your belt."

He stood up with his bucket and grinned at her over the back of his cow. "It's all your fault. If you weren't such a good cook—I mean, such a plain cook."

"Go get the milk cans ready. I'll take them to the collection station while you are gone."

"Do you have help there to empty them?"

"I do. Get busy and stop asking so many questions, or you won't get any breakfast."

"Yes, ma'am. My lips are sealed now. Not another question. No siree. Quiet as a mouse from now until you're done cooking." He drew his thumb and forefinger across his lips.

She shook her head at his foolishness and went to the house. If she was quick, she could make the biscuits he liked so well. It was fun cooking for a man who enjoyed what she made as much as Tully did. He never left the table without giving her a compliment.

She was pulling the pan of biscuits out of the oven when he came in. His eyes lit up like those of a child getting a lollipop. He walked over and snatched one from her pan. He stepped back, tossing it from hand to hand. "Hot, hot, hot."

"Serves you right. Wash up and then see if Gideon needs any help."

He dropped the biscuit on his plate and did as she asked. When he came back with Gideon at his side and Annabeth riding piggyback, Becca smiled to herself.

He was a good and kind man. What he needed was a family of his own.

He pulled out Gideon's chair and then swung Annabeth around and planted her on the floor by the table. She looked at Becca with wide eyes. "*Mamm*, Tully is going to take me to school. *Daadi* said that was okay. Is it?"

"It is, but you will not make a habit of it."

"I know. Tully said he could take us into Fort Craig to do some shopping if you want to go later this week."

Becca considered the offer. "I do need to pick up baking supplies and fabric. Gideon, do you need anything?"

"Razor blades. I have three left, so there is no rush."

Tully sat down beside Gideon. "You go to all the trouble of shaving your mustache and cheeks but keep your chin whiskers. Why? If you don't mind my asking."

Gideon rubbed his knuckles over his cheek. "Because this is our way. This was how my father and grandfather did it. That is reason enough."

"Got it. I was thinking it might mean something special."

"Eva may know, for she has studied books about our past," Becca said. "An Amish man grows a beard only after he marries. In our church he may trim his beard after his first child is born. All married Amish men have beards, but not all churches allow them to be trimmed."

Tully folded his hands together and closed his eyes. "For such plain folks, you sure have some complicated traditions."

She peeked at him twice before Gideon signaled the prayer was done by asking for his eggs. Tully never looked up. He wore a faint frown as if he were concentrating on doing something difficult. Maybe praying was difficult for him, but she was pleased to see he was trying. Perhaps Pastor Frank would be able to help Tully find his way back to God.

The following days fell into the same pattern. She started to forget he wasn't part of her family. They did their chores together; he teased her. He kept Gideon entertained with games of checkers or stories. The days were short but comfortable as he became familiar with her routine. He brought in wood before she had to ask. He even scrubbed the milk pails in the mornings before she was up, and he never forgot to thank her for a delicious meal.

On Thursday evening Michael and Bethany stopped in for a visit along with baby Eli, Bethany's younger brother Ivan and her sister Jenny. At fifteen, Ivan was a gangly youth with a dry wit and a sharp mind. He had lots of questions for Tully about ranching and admitted he had thought of settling in Montana in one of the new Amish communities there.

The bishop arrived a short time later to check on Gideon. Michael announced he wanted a chance to even the score with Tully over their game of horseshoes and suggested a game of checkers. Tully grinned and turned to the bishop. "What about it? Are you up for a match or two, as well?"

Bishop Schultz hooked his thumbs through his suspenders and rocked back on his heels. "I like a good game now and then."

Gideon laughingly brought out the set.

Jenny, Bethany and Becca retreated to the kitchen to visit while Annabeth played with the baby on a quilt on the floor. Bethany cast a glance down the hall. "Tully seems to be enjoying the evening."

She heard a shout of laughter from the living room and smiled. "It sounds like he's having a very *goot* time tonight. He certainly enjoyed himself on Sunday thanks to Michael and Jesse."

"What are you planning for him next?"

"I'm hoping more of our friends will come to visit Gideon and Tully this next week. Please pass that along. The cookie exchange party is at the Lapp home next Saturday. The following Tuesday is our caroling. You're coming, right?"

"Of course," Bethany assured her.

"Is Pastor Frank taking a group to the parade in Presque Isle again?" Becca asked.

"He is. That's on Wednesday the twenty-third."

"We will join him if there is room for us. If not, Tully can drive his car. That leaves the school Christmas program for last. Annabeth is dying to have Tully see her in the play."

"That should make a wonderful Christmas holiday for anyone."

"I hope so." Becca glanced down the hall to where the men were laughing again. She wanted Tully to feel welcome in her community. Her friends were making that happen.

Tully beat Michael and the bishop soundly at checkers. He moved aside to let Michael take on Gideon in the next game as the bishop gathered up his things. "Walk me out, Tully."

"Sure." They passed through the kitchen, where the bishop bid Becca good-night, and the two men stepped out onto the porch. It was a cold, crisp night. The stars glittering overhead gave enough light to see by.

"It was a good game," Tully said. He struggled for a moment to put into words how the Sunday service had affected him. "I wanted you to know I enjoyed the part of your preaching and the service I caught the other morning. It was moving. I don't know much about the Amish, but I can see your faith is deep. I envy the serenity you all seem to have."

"*Gott*'s love knows no bounds. Faith and peacefulness are available to every man who seeks Him. Not just the Amish."

Tully let the bishop's words sink in. Could he find the same kind of relationship with God? Was he ready to seek that? Maybe he was.

The bishop looked at him for a long moment. "How are you getting along with Gideon and Becca?"

Tully grinned. "They are wonderful people. *Kind* doesn't begin to describe them. However, I didn't expect the work to be so hard. I don't know how the two of them have managed alone."

"It's true that Gideon has struggled with his health. It would be best if Becca married again."

Was that a hint? Tully wasn't sure where the man was going. "She would make any fellow a fine wife."

"Any Amish man," the bishop said with a pointed look at Tully. "Becca can't marry outside our faith. It is forbidden. If she were to do such a thing, she would be shunned by all the faithful who know and love her."

Tully kept his face expressionless. It was a hint, just not the kind he'd expected. "I wasn't aware of that rule. I can assure you Becca has shown me only kindness."

"I never doubted that, but kindness can sometimes be mistaken for affection of a different nature."

Tully shoved his hands in the pockets of his coat. "I get your drift. You don't have to worry. I will be moving on soon enough."

"My aim isn't to drive you away, Tully Lange. You are welcome in this community and have made many *goot* friends already. It is an unusual thing for an *Englisch* fellow to accomplish, but I have seen how you look at her. You care for her. My purpose in speaking thus is to prevent needless pain for you and for Becca."

Tully pressed his lips together tightly and mustered as much dignity as he could. "I appreciate that, sir. I do."

The bishop left, taking with him any faint hopes that Tully harbored about building a relationship with Becca.

So what now? What should he do? If the bishop could read Tully's feelings for her so easily, maybe others could, too.

The answer was painfully obvious. He would do nothing. Her family and her faith were everything to Becca. He could never ask her to give them up.

He would remain friends with her and her family until he left, but he would never forget the way she made him feel.

On the following day, Becca noticed Tully was quieter than usual, but he offered to drive Annabeth to school again and she agreed. That evening after the chores were done and both Gideon and Annabeth had gone to bed, Becca noticed a light coming from beneath the door to the living room. Thinking that Gideon must have left it on, she went in to turn it off and saw Tully reading in Gideon's favorite chair. He looked up when she came in.

He gestured to the propane lamp above his head. "This is much brighter than the one in my room. I hope you don't mind."

"Of course not. What are you reading?"

"A book Annabeth's teacher loaned me today. It's about the beginnings of the Amish church. Those early Amish sure had it rough."

"They did. Their martyrdom still inspires us to remain true to our faith in spite of any obstacle."

"I can see why you're a peace-loving bunch."

"Because violence only begets violence. We must turn the other cheek and forgive those that would harm us."

"From a soldier's point of view, I always thought the threat of force was the best way to keep the peace. There are things worth fighting for. I would've dealt harshly with the men who persecuted your ancestors."

"Vengeance belongs to *Gott*. Only He knows what is in a man's heart. Good men can do evil things, and evil men can do good things. It is not for us to judge which is which."

"Doesn't it bother you that someone can get away with cruel deeds and even murder?"

"*Gott* can mete out a punishment that is everlasting. Just because the scales are not balanced in our sight does not mean they are not balanced."

"Food for thought. Oh, I found out why Amish men don't have mustaches. Apparently the mustache was a symbol of the military in bygone days. Rather than be associated with that, the Amish chose to shave their mustaches but leave their beards."

"I did not know that. It is just something that has always been done."

He stared down at the book in his hands. "I learned that an Amish person can't marry outside the faith. Are there any exceptions?"

Her heart dropped. He hadn't known why she couldn't return his affection. Now he would understand, and perhaps things could be easier between them. "There are no exceptions."

His lips twisted into a wry smile. "It's good to know it wasn't just me."

She heard the catch in his voice. He had hoped for another answer. She clenched her hands together to keep from reaching for him. "You are a fine man, Tully, but you are not Amish. The Lord has someone in mind for you. I'm sure of it."

His gaze slid away from her back to his book. "Thanks. *Guten naucht*, Becca."

She left the room and closed the door softly. She entered her bedroom and sat on the edge of her bed. She liked him tremendously. She could easily find herself falling for him if she wasn't careful. He wasn't a little boy in need of a bright Christmas season, he was an outsider. An *Englischer* who would leave soon. She couldn't lose sight of that fact, no matter how much she came to care for him.

After a restless night, she resolved to treat Tully as she would any other visitor to her home. She bade him good morning and set about getting ready to do the chores. He seemed subdued, as well. Neither of them spoke much as they took care of the cattle and returned to the house. They washed up side by side at the sink. Finally she couldn't stand the silence from her usually talkative friend. She glanced his way. "Is something wrong?"

"I was about to ask you the same thing."

She couldn't lie to him, but she didn't have to tell him the whole truth. "I didn't sleep well last night."

"Me neither." Their eyes met, and he looked away.

"Is something troubling you?" Why did she ask when she wasn't sure she wanted to hear the answer?

"Nothing specific. I'm going to need to find a paying job after Christmas, and a place to live. I hate to rely on my friend until I can start making ends meet." He shrugged. "All little stuff. At least no one is shooting at me."

Why did he have to start joking when he was talking about leaving? Her intention to treat him like any other visitor evaporated into thin air. Sadness brought the sting of tears to the back of her eyes. "I will miss you when you leave, Tully Lange."

The smile on his face slowly faded as he gazed at her. "Will you?"

He took a step closer. The air in the kitchen seemed to thicken around her, bringing a strange warmth to her skin as she stared into his dark eyes. "So very much," she whispered.

He reached out and drew his fingers along the curve of her jaw. She closed her eyes and leaned into his gentle touch.

Chapter Thirteen

Tully wanted to kiss Becca's sweet lips but knew he couldn't. His pounding heart said *go for it*, but his conscience shouted that it would be wrong. She was a vulnerable woman dealing with a host of worries. He was here to help, not to add to her troubles. No drink had ever been this hard to pass up. Learning that she couldn't marry an outsider had left him tossing and turning for the past two nights. He longed to be a part of her life, but that was forbidden to her. She would never be his.

He bent and pressed his lips to her forehead.

Her eyes flew open. He saw confusion and then shame. She pressed her hands to her cheeks as they blossomed bright red.

She turned away from him. "What you must think of me."

"Only good things. Too good for the likes of me."

"I'm so ashamed."

"Don't be. We are both tired. Our emotions got carried away. You have nothing to be sorry for."

She heard Gideon coming down the hall. She turned

toward the window so he couldn't see her face. Tully busied himself finding a clean pair of gloves from the drawer near the front door.

Gideon paused in the doorway. "Do you know how to drive a horse, Cowboy?"

Tully looked up. "Becca gave me a lesson the other day, but I'm hardly an expert. I think the horse knew what he was doing more than I did."

"Why don't you go with Becca to the milk collection station so you can take over that chore while you are here?"

"Okay." Tully glanced at Becca. She wouldn't look at him.

Becca wiped her hands on her apron. "There is *kaffee* on the stove. Do you want a cup before I leave, Gideon?"

"*Danki*. How are my cows?"

She pulled a white mug from the cupboard and filled it. "Fine. Eating well and giving between two and a half and three gallons of milk each."

"So much? No wonder Tully's arms could use a rest."

Tully rubbed his forearms and managed a half-hearted grin. "That ain't no lie."

Gideon accepted the cup from Becca. "You will toughen up in a few more days. You have done well. Much better than I expected when you first offered to stay. He has made a *goot* dairyman, hasn't he, Becca?"

"Very *goot*." Becca went toward the door. "We need to get going."

"Right." Tully settled his hat on his head and followed her outside.

She kept her gaze averted as they trudged through the snow to the barn. He didn't like the tenseness between them, but he wasn't sure how to overcome it. He'd messed up again big-time. How was he going to fix this?

When they had Cupcake, the big gray mare, hitched to the wagon, Tully offered his hand to help Becca up to the high seat. She ignored it and scrambled up by herself. He joined her, all the while wishing he hadn't put them in such an awkward position. Becca picked up the driving lines, and Cupcake headed for the highway with a word from her.

They rode in silence through the snow-covered countryside dotted with pine forests, open fields and farms with red barns trimmed in white. "It's pretty country," he said when the silence dragged on too long.

She didn't reply. After a few more minutes, he couldn't take it anymore. "You're going to have to speak to me sometime."

"Not if I can help it."

It wasn't much, but it was a start. "I stepped over the line back there, and I'm sorry. It won't happen again."

"It can't, Tully. You know why."

"Sure. Because I'm not one of you."

She looked at him then. "I care about you, Tully, but I can never act on those feelings. You must understand. I'm sorry if anything I did led you to believe otherwise."

He wanted to make a joke about it, get her to smile at him, but he couldn't find the humor in his heartache. "I made the mistake, Becca. You didn't do anything wrong. You, Annabeth and Gideon, you have become the closest thing to a family that I've known since I was a boy. I don't want to lose your friendship, but I'll understand if you want me to leave."

Becca cast a sidelong glance at Tully as she bit her lower lip. It might be for the best, but she didn't want him to go. He would be leaving soon enough. He had become so dear to her. She wanted to cherish every minute of his company. The memories would have to last a lifetime. "You may stay as you had planned. We do need your help."

"Does this mean you and I can be friends again? Are we okay?"

"Our friendship was never in jeopardy." That was true. It was her heart that worried her. And his.

"I'm so relieved to hear you say that." He nudged her shoulder with his. She looked his way and saw he was grinning. "You have no idea how much I would miss your cooking."

He was always ready with a joke. She shook her head, but she couldn't hold back a smile. "You and your stomach."

He gestured ahead of them. "If you'd missed as many meals as I have, you'd understand. Is that big barn up ahead where we're going?"

"It is. You will have to drive straight into the barn on the south end. Usually the doors are open. If they aren't, there is a telephone on the wall you can use to call the main house."

"How many cows do they milk?"

"About a hundred."

"I'm going to guess they have electric milking machines. Do you think they would rent us a couple? I could figure out how to run an extension cord from one of your English neighbors. It could cut our work-load in half."

She knew he was trying to lighten the mood and put them back on their old footing. "Hard work never hurt anyone, Tully."

"Says the woman who doesn't know how easy elec-tricity makes everything. You know, I still try to turn on the light switch when I walk into my bedroom, only there is no light switch. How long do you think before I learn not to do that?"

"We stayed at a motel in Florida for a month, and I never once turned on the light."

"And that in a nutshell is the difference between us," he said softly, making her look his way. "I need lights to see what is in front of my face. You don't. Looks like the barn doors are closed. Where is the phone?"

Tully's knees were shaking when he got down from the wagon. He stumbled a little on his first step. He wasn't sure that he had repaired his relationship with Becca, but at least she was speaking to him and hadn't told him to leave. She blamed herself for his behav-ior. She couldn't be more wrong. It had been his mis-take. The need to have a drink and forget his stupidity hit him like a hammer. He licked his dry lips and told himself it wouldn't help. He'd still be a fool where she was concerned.

After they unloaded the milk, Becca handed Tully the lines when he climbed aboard. The big horse am-bled toward home at his command.

Becca sat quietly beside him, occasionally giving him small pointers about his driving. He couldn't keep his mind on what he was doing. The more he tried to push the idea of having a drink out of his mind, the bigger it became.

Once they reached home, he put Cupcake away and went to split wood until he had a stack as high as he could reach in the woodshed. When Becca called him in for lunch, he forced himself to smile and joke with her and Gideon. He could see in her eyes that things still were not right between them, but they were both making an effort to appear normal. Fake it until you make it, as Arnie had said.

"Do you think you can drive me into Fort Craig this afternoon?" Becca asked.

He nodded. "Sure. I know Annabeth would like to go along."

Becca smiled tentatively. "I was about to suggest it."

Tully looked to Gideon. "Do you want to come?"

"Becca knows what brand of razor blades I use. I see no need to go with you. Becca, give the man his salary. He has earned it."

Becca went to the cupboard and brought down a mason jar where she deposited their payments from the milk bank. She pulled out several bills and held them toward Tully.

Shocked, he put both hands up. "No, that was not the arrangement. I work for room and board. I probably should pay you because of how much I eat."

"A worker is worthy of his hire," Gideon said. "We can't afford much, but we share what we have. Take it and be done."

Tully could tell by the man's set features that he wasn't going to take no for an answer. "Thank you. I appreciate it. Now I can put gas in the car, and Becca won't have to push it home from town."

Gideon snorted. "A horse doesn't run out of gas. You should take the buggy."

"My car has a good heater. Hot bricks under your feet are okay, but the inside of a buggy is pretty cold when it is only twenty degrees outside."

"The *Englisch* are a soft bunch," Gideon said. "Becca, is there *kaffee*?"

With the outing to look forward to, thoughts of finding a drink somewhere decreased in Tully's mind. He was going to town with a little money in his pocket. The day was beginning to look up.

Annabeth came out of the house and gave a shout of joy when she saw Tully's car parked in front of the gate. "Are we going to Fort Craig?"

He held open the back door for her. "Yes, we are. Your mother has shopping she needs to do."

Annabeth jumped up and down in front of him. "I love going to town. Do you think they will have the Christmas lights up?"

"Christmas is only two weeks away, so I'm sure they will. But you won't get to see them unless you get in the car."

She scurried in, and he closed the door behind her. He got in, as well. Becca turned around in her seat to look at Annabeth. "We can't stay late. We have to get back in time to milk."

"I know that it will be fun anyway. I'm going to tell everybody the story of our trip at school on Monday."

Tully caught Becca's gaze. She arched one eyebrow at him. "My daughter is becoming another storyteller in the family. This is your fault."

"I will take credit for that. Tell me all the things you

see along the way, Annabeth, and then you will remember them when you get to school next week."

As Annabeth chattered happily from the back seat with her face glued to the passenger-side window, Tully drove slowly, glad that he was able to give the child a special outing. He was glad, too, that her mother was along. If he behaved, he and Becca could stay friends. He wanted that more than anything. It hurt that their relationship could never grow into anything more, but he would cherish the time he had left with her.

On his way through town, his eyes were drawn to the Lumberjack Bar. It was Saturday. People were off work for the weekend. The parking lot was already half-full of cars. There would be friends sharing a few beers, others drinking alone.

"Tully, look out!"

Becca's cry jerked his attention back to the road, where a truck was stopped at the light in front of them. He hit the brakes and managed to avoid rear-ending the vehicle. "Sorry. I guess I've gotten rusty at driving."

"Eyes on the road at all times," Annabeth said. "I learned that in school."

He looked in the rearview mirror. "Are you taking driver's education?"

"*Nee*, I'm too little, but Otto and the twins are."

He cocked his head toward Becca. "Seriously?"

"We share the road with all kinds of traffic. We obey the same rules. Our children must learn to be safe drivers in their buggies and wagons. Unlike an *Englisch* cowboy that I know. The light is green."

He drove on and parked in front of the grocery store at her direction. "Shouldn't we get groceries last? You don't want anything to spoil."

She pointed to a local bank sign. The time, followed

by "22 degrees," scrolled across it. "It's the middle of December in northern Maine. The inside of your car will be colder than my refrigerator by the time we finish."

"Right. What was I thinking?"

Becca produced a list. "I will need two carts. I have a lot of baking to do."

She wasn't kidding. They left the building with enough flour, sugar and whatnot to fill his trunk. They gathered a few stares along the way. He wasn't sure if it was because of her Amish clothing or because she was with a man who wasn't Amish. As they walked down the sidewalk to the fabric store, he began to get annoyed with the number of people gawking at them while Annabeth and Becca were pointing out the lights and window displays they liked.

"Why do these people think it's okay to stare at you?" he asked.

"We are an oddity here. It's not like Pennsylvania, where the Amish are everywhere."

"It's rude. I'd like to tell some of them to mind their manners."

"Then you would be the impolite one. We pay them no mind."

It was good advice, but he couldn't shake the feeling that people were judging them for their lifestyle. It was a familiar feeling that he didn't like. He used to try to blur out the faces of the people looking down on him when he was homeless and panhandling for enough cash to get a few drinks. "It isn't right."

Becca didn't understand why Tully was angry with the onlookers. She and Annabeth had learned to ignore stares from an early age. "Tully, it's fine."

"It isn't." He glared at two shoppers in the fabric store. They moved away.

She decided the material for a new dress could wait until another time. "I'm ready to go home."

"Buy what you came for. Don't let these people ruin your outing."

At the sound of his raised voice, Annabeth pressed close to Becca's side. She put her arm around her daughter. "They aren't the ones making us uncomfortable, Tully."

He looked at her with a puzzled expression. "I am?"

"Please, let's go."

He seemed confused. "Sure. I'm sorry. I wanted you to have a nice time with me this afternoon."

"We have had a *goot* time, haven't we, Annabeth? We got to see lots of Christmas decorations and the pretty window displays, but it's time to get back."

"I'll go get the car." He walked away without waiting for her answer.

"What's Tully upset about, *Mamm*?"

"I'm not sure, honey, but he isn't upset with you. Okay?"

"Is he mad because we're Amish?"

"*Nee.* He doesn't understand our ways, that's all."

"I wish he did."

"So do I." Something was troubling him. She didn't think it was their conversation from earlier. Would he confide in her? Should she ask?

He arrived with the car. They got in, and he headed out of town. When he stopped at the traffic light, she noticed he was staring at a business just off the highway. She took a second look and realized it was a bar. A place that served alcohol. What was his interest in a place like that? She turned her face away from it. "The light is green, Tully."

"What? Oh yeah. Thanks."

He remained silent until they reached the house, but his mood did improve as he helped her carry in her groceries. "This can't all be for me. I know I don't eat that much."

"It's for my Christmas baking."

"I hope I get to sample some."

She smiled to reassure him. "You will."

Afterward, they finished the chores, and she made a light supper. Tully was unusually quiet during the meal. Gideon seemed to notice. He raised his brow at her. She gave a slight shake of her head. As soon as the table was cleared, Tully disappeared into his room and came out twenty minutes later dressed in the Western shirt and jeans he had worn to church. He had polished his boots.

He took his coat and hat off the peg and put them on. "I'm going out for a while. Don't wait up for me."

"All right." She stared at the door as it closed behind him, wondering where he was going and why she was suddenly afraid he wouldn't come back.

Tully drove into Fort Craig again, pulled into the familiar parking lot and got out. He drew a deep breath of the cold air. He walked to the rear of the building and went down the steps leading to a basement. Above the door of what looked like a classroom was a hand-lettered sign that said Welcome to a Safe Place. Pastor Frank stood beside the door with a kindly smile on his face. "Are you here for the meeting?"

Tully held out his hand. "Hello. My name is Tully

and I'm an alcoholic in recovery. I've been sober for four months and nineteen days."

"Welcome, Tully. Come in and meet our other members."

Tully followed Frank into the classroom. Four men and two women were seated on folding chairs in a circle. He was relieved to see Michael wasn't among them. One of the men got up and added another chair to the circle for Tully. He sat down and rubbed his sweaty palms on his jeans.

Pastor Frank added another chair and sat down. "Let's get started. I'm Frank, and I'm an alcoholic. I've been sober for twenty-two years and nine months."

"Welcome, Frank," everyone said.

The anxiety that plagued Tully slowly seeped away. He needed to be here. He listened in amazement to the stories of the other members, some of whom, like Frank, had been sober for more than two decades. One young woman had been sober for six days. Her hands were still trembling. The understanding and compassion of those around him buoyed his spirits and strengthened his resolve to stay sober.

When the meeting was over, Pastor Frank came over and offered his hand. "It was good of you to join us. If you need to talk to someone, I'm always available."

"Thanks, that means a lot."

Later, when Tully quietly let himself into Becca's house, he was shocked to see her still up. She looked relieved to see him. He didn't understand why. He had given her one rough day. "I thought I told you not to wait up."

It warmed his heart that she had.

She gestured toward a pile of gray cloth on the table.

"I had some sewing to finish. Annabeth's shepherdess costume. They're having dress rehearsals this week. Did you have a nice time tonight?"

She might be angling for information about where he had been, but she was being polite about it. He wasn't ready to reveal his addiction to her. Their conversation that morning and their trip into town had made him painfully aware that he had a lot of work to do on handling difficult situations. If only he could learn her calm acceptance. "I met with some new friends. I don't think you would know them. They aren't Amish."

"You must have a lot of friends who aren't Amish."

He hung up his hat and coat and then crossed the room to stand beside her. "I don't have many friends at all, but the one I value most does happen to be Amish." He leaned close without touching her. "I'm fortunate that she has a forgiving nature along with being a wonderful cook."

She drew back to stare at him. "Are you trying to flatter me again?"

"Nope. I know that is not your way. I'm being truthful. I'm sorry for ruining the trip to town for you and Annabeth." He longed to caress her face, but he knew it would only lead to more awkwardness between them.

A little smile tipped up the corner of her mouth right where he wanted to plant a kiss. "It wasn't ruined. Only a tiny bit raveled at the edges."

"Are you trying to be funny?"

"I am. How am I doing?"

"Needs work."

"Speaking of work, Gabe will be here in the morning to help you milk. I have things in the house to do."

"Does it involve cooking?" he asked hopefully.

"Cooking and baking."

"In that case, you should get to bed. You need your rest."

She grew serious as a frown creased her brow. "I was afraid you weren't coming back."

He pushed his hands deep in his pockets. "I'm sorry you thought that."

"Promise you won't leave without saying goodbye."

"I promise."

Her expression cleared. "All right. *Guten naucht,* Cowboy."

He smiled softly at her. She was so easy to love. "*Guten naucht, Frau* Beachy."

He watched her walk out of the kitchen and raked one hand through his hair. He wasn't Amish, but was there any way to remain a part of her life? What if he stayed in the area? They could still be friends. He could see her now and again, but he knew it wouldn't work.

He would be doomed to love her from afar, because he was in love with her. How could he bear that?

Chapter Fourteen

Becca grew concerned about Tully. Although she couldn't say that he had been secretive about his trip into Fort Craig, she knew he hadn't told her everything. She didn't have a right to pry into his private life, but that didn't keep her from wanting to know where he had gone.

When he came into breakfast the next morning, he seemed like his old self, cheerful and smiling. He apologized to Annabeth and promised he would take her to town again soon. Her daughter seemed satisfied with that and chatted happily with him. Tully had a way of making her little girl adore him.

Becca glanced at the clock on the wall. "Gabe should be here soon. Annabeth, I have a chore for you. I want you to help your grandfather shell pecans. We are baking our gift boxes to give to the nursing homes this morning." It was the off Sunday, and her friends would be over to help with the baking. None of them viewed it as extra work on the day of rest. It would be a fun-filled day, with visiting, laughter and perhaps even singing.

"But I wanted to make Christmas cards today," Annabeth said.

"I won't have time to help you. We can do that on Monday after school."

"I can help her," Tully offered.

"All right. After the chores are done, the two of you can set up a table in the living room and make cards there."

She heard the arrival of the first buggy and looked out. It was Dinah and Gemma. She turned to Tully. "Will you stable the horses for our company? It's too cold to leave them standing outside."

"I'll take care of them." He went out the door with the milking pails.

As more women showed up, Becca became immersed in measuring, mixing and baking, and enjoying the company of her friends. The kitchen became so warm they were forced to open the window. When Tully returned from the milk delivery, he stopped in the open doorway with a stunned expression on his face. "When you said you had a little baking to do, you weren't kidding. It smells great in here."

All eight women turned to greet him and began offering him samples of what had been made. Becca paid close attention to what he liked the best so she could make more for him later. Everything today was going into gift boxes to be delivered to the three nursing homes in the county.

Gideon pushed two large bowls of shelled pecans toward Dinah. "That's the last of them. I'll be in the living room if you need me."

Tully, who was sampling a thumbprint cookie,

walked to Becca's side. "I'll crack nuts if you bring me cookies to sample."

She gave him a gentle push toward the hallway. "Get out of my kitchen and out of my way. Annabeth is waiting for you in the living room."

"That's just cruel. There are at least five types of cookies I haven't tried yet."

"I'll save you some of mine," Gemma said.

"Did you make the chocolate chip–oatmeal ones?" He looked hopefully at the box she was packing.

"I made the snickerdoodles." She handed him one.

"Thanks." He took a bite and moaned. "Becca, you have a rival. Gemma, you wouldn't by chance need a hired man who works for room and board, would you? I think I'm free after Christmas."

Becca pointed to the hall. "You will find yourself free before that if you don't get out of the way."

He held up both hands and ambled out of the room. Gemma chuckled. "He's such a fun fellow. Is there any chance he will stay in our community?"

Becca sighed. "I don't think so. He hasn't mentioned any such plan." Caring for him the way she did and not being able to share those feelings would be hard if he stayed, but she didn't want him to leave.

An hour later she went to check on Annabeth's progress with her Christmas cards. She found Tully and her daughter sprawled on the wood floor with scraps of ribbon, paper cutouts and construction paper spread all around them. Gideon was dozing in his chair. Tully laid two scraps of ribbon on a piece of paper that was already adorned with the picture of a lamb. "What do you think? The green or the blue?"

Annabeth studied his composition. "I think the green."

"Glue." He held out his hand. She placed a bottle in it. He applied one drop carefully and handed it back. "Who does this card go to?"

"Teacher Eva."

He wrote the name on the envelope and added it to a small stack near his elbow. "Now what?"

"Can you draw a camel?" she asked.

"Maybe. Who are you sending this one to?"

"To Otto."

"In that case, I think my camel will be good enough." He glanced up at Becca. "May we help you?"

"I have made sandwiches for lunch. Come and have some when you get hungry."

He scrambled to his feet. "I'm always hungry."

"Would you bring me one, Tully?" Annabeth asked.

"Sure." He stopped beside Becca. "How goes the monster bake?"

"We're almost done. You're good to spend time with her."

"You have a great kid, in case no one has told you that."

"*Danki.*"

"But then, she has a wonderful mother, so it shouldn't be any surprise." He curled his fingers around her hand and gave a brief squeeze before he left the room.

Becca kept her composure with difficulty. Theirs was a hopeless situation, but she cherished the tenderness of his touch.

"I like him, *Mamm*," Annabeth said.

"So do I."

She would miss Tully when he left, but she suspected

her daughter would miss him just as much, if not more. She straightened. Her goal was to give Tully a Christmas season to remember them by, but she would always treasure their time together.

After the baking party left and the chores were done that evening, she sat listening to Gideon read to them from the Bible as Annabeth and Tully finished her daughter's cards. She glanced Tully's way and caught him watching her with such sadness in his eyes that she longed to comfort him. But she couldn't. Because she wanted to be held in his arms and be comforted, too. Somehow, she had to make it until Christmas without giving in to that desire. For if he held her, she wasn't sure she could let him go.

Tully wasn't going to be able to walk away from Becca and her family. He knew it deep in his heart. He took a long, hard look at the path before him and wondered if it was even possible. On Monday morning when Becca took Annabeth to school, he joined Gideon in the living room.

Tully sat in the chair across from him and drew a deep breath. "Gideon, how does someone become Amish? I mean, if you're not born to Amish parents, is there an entrance exam of some kind?"

Gideon was silent for several long seconds. "We do not seek converts from outside our church. We accept that our way is not for everyone. Very few people have converted to the Amish faith. I personally do not know of anyone who has done so."

"But it is possible?"

"Possible, but I would think very difficult. To be Amish is something you are raised with. Why we dress and speak the way we do. Our rejection of higher education, even the meaning behind the songs we sing at our church service. Those are things most outsiders can't understand. Why do you ask?"

"Your people seem so content with their lives. That's a rare thing."

"Is it? Why?"

"I don't know. I guess most folks want to get ahead. They want to have more for themselves and for their children. They want a better job or to make more money, have a bigger house or own a fancier car. If they can't make that happen, they feel cheated."

"Are you one of those people? Are you discontent with your life?"

"There are a lot of things I don't like about my life." The fact that he had wasted two long years in a nearly continuous alcoholic stupor was one of them. The fact that his addiction had gotten his best friend killed was another.

"If you don't like something, can't you change it?"

"I'm working on that, but some things can't be changed." What would Gideon think if he told the man he was an alcoholic? Would he even understand what that meant?

"All things are possible with God. Perhaps you should ask for His help."

"I'm pretty sure He has better things to do than help a down-and-out cowboy."

"God does not love one of his children more than another. He has compassion for all. We Amish believe worship is important and that we are following the path He has laid out for us, but we are not more beloved in

His sight than anyone else. To assume that we are would be the worst form of *hohchmoot*."

"That means arrogance or conceit, right?"

"*Ja*, pride. *Gelassenheit*, humility, must be present in all aspects of our lives. We must be humble, quiet, submissive to the will of *Gott*. The *Englisch* admire our way of living, but very few can follow in our footsteps."

"But if someone wanted to live as you do, they could become Amish, right?"

"It would be better to live as we do and remain *Englisch*. This is about your feelings for Becca, isn't it? I'm old, but I'm not blind."

Tully felt the heat rush to his face and had to admit the truth. "I'm in love with her, Gideon." A weight lifted from his shoulders at being able to say it out loud.

"Have you told her this?"

"No. She may suspect, but I haven't said anything. I didn't know a relationship with her wasn't possible until the night the bishop came to play checkers. He's also older but not blind."

"Tully, Becca can't be the reason you look to join our faith. It must be because *Gott* has led you to that point, otherwise it is a meaningless gesture."

"It's about more than my feelings for her. I love it here. I have never felt as much at home as I do with you, Becca, Annabeth and the friends I've made here. I want to keep all of you in my life. This isn't a whim. I've been studying some books Eva gave me. Tell me how to take the next step. If God wants me on this path, He will guide me the rest of the way."

Tully was a little shocked by how much he believed what he just said. There was no denying that God had brought him here.

Gideon was silent for a long moment. "Talk to Bishop Schultz about this, but do not speak to Becca of your feelings. You are forbidden to her. It breaks my heart to say this, for I like you, Tully, and I see that she cares about you, too, but this is the way it must be."

"Okay. I'd like to attend services with you this coming Sunday."

"You are welcome to do so. If the bishop agrees, perhaps he will allow you to start instructions."

If God had a plan for him, Tully was going to open his heart and listen.

Becca joined Tully in the barn that evening, and they fell into their old rhythm of working alongside each other without saying much. It was comfortable in the barn. The troubles of the outside world were left behind as they cared for the cattle, horses and little Diamond. In their secluded world, they didn't have to worry about doing or saying the wrong thing in front of Gideon or Annabeth. Tully was quieter, but he seemed content. She was happy just to be with him. The awkwardness between them had vanished.

Over the course of the week, many of their friends came to visit in the evenings, as she had hoped, leaving less time for her and Tully to be alone. It was a good thing. She was able to keep a lid on her growing feelings for him. She enjoyed watching his interactions with Danny, Jesse, Michael and the Fisher brothers. They all liked his company. He was endearing, not just to her but to everyone he met. If it sometimes felt like Tully was withdrawing from her, she accepted that he needed the distance as much as she did.

When they didn't have company, Tully and Gideon

spent time discussing the Bible and talking about the foundations of the Amish church. Tully was truly interested in learning about their faith. Sometimes she joined the discussion. It provided a balm to her aching heart knowing Tully was seeking to understand God's word.

The cookie exchange party on Saturday turned out to be the highlight of a bittersweet week for her as she watched him laughing and interacting with everyone in the community. Annabeth was never far from his side.

Tully carried her sleeping daughter against his shoulder when they finally got home. Gideon bade them good-night and went to his room. She went ahead of Tully down the hall to Annabeth's room, opened the door and turned down the bed. He laid her child down gently without waking her. Together they took off her coat and her shoes.

Tully stepped back as Becca unpinned Annabeth's hair and pulled the quilt over her shoulders.

"Thank you, Becca."

She looked up. "For what?"

"For this. For a chance to feel like I'm part of a real family again. It's been wonderful. *Wunderbar*, as you say."

"I'm glad." It was what she had wanted for him, so why did it make her want to cry?

"I'm coming to the church service with you tomorrow."

"I thought you would be going to Pastor Frank's church again."

"I don't think that's where I'm meant to be. I know it's not where I want to be. I plan to speak to the bishop about joining the church. I know he must agree before I can take instructions."

She pressed a hand to the sudden ache in her chest. Tully was willing to become Amish?

She wouldn't get her hopes up. It was a difficult undertaking. She'd only heard of a few people who had come into the church from the outside. "If that is what God wants for you, I will be glad."

"I told Gideon I hadn't said anything, but I think you know how I feel about you."

She held a hand to his lips. "Don't. Please."

What if Tully couldn't do it? What if the newness of these weeks wore off and he said goodbye anyway? It didn't bear thinking about. Knowing she could never be his was better than believing she could be and having that dream crushed.

He pulled her hand away and kissed her palm. "I won't until I have the right to speak what's in my heart. Good night, Becca." He turned and walked out of the room.

The next morning Tully took his place on the back row of benches beside Otto, hoping the boy would help him out again when he couldn't understand the preaching. To his surprise, Gabe and Danny sat down on either side of him as Otto made room for them.

"What are you doing here, Cowboy?" Danny asked.

"I've come to worship. You?" He glanced between both men.

"The same, but we belong here," Gabe said.

"You are fortunate men. I'm still looking for the place where I belong." He gazed at Becca sitting near the front.

"And you think it might be with us?" Danny asked, rubbing his chin thoughtfully.

"It seems to me the Lord went to a lot of trouble to get me here. I'm going to give Him a chance to show me why."

"He could be right," Gabe said, looking across Tully to Danny. "We cannot know the mind of *Gott*."

Tully had learned to ask for help with his addiction. This was every bit as important to him. "I admit I'm a fish out of water here. Any advice you fellas can give me will be deeply appreciated."

"Are you sure this is what you want?" Gabe asked.

"Yes."

"Okay," Danny said. "You'll need to learn the language. I can help with that."

Tully rubbed his palms on his pant legs. "First I need to speak with the bishop. He has to agree."

"He isn't here today," Danny said. "Bishop Bontrager from Whitefield is taking his place."

That wasn't what Tully wanted to hear. "When will Bishop Schultz be back?"

Gabe clapped a hand on Tully's shoulder. "Tomorrow. He plans to go caroling with us. You can speak to him then."

They sat straighter as the bishop and ministers came in. Gabe handed Tully a songbook. He opened it and followed along, adding his voice to those raised in praise. The peace he had sensed the first time settled over him again. He realized it was the presence of God.

The day for caroling arrived with a light snowfall in the morning that tapered off by noon, leaving a fresh coat of white on the countryside. Annabeth could barely contain her excitement when she got home from school.

"Tully, hurry up," she called from her place on the

back seat of the sleigh. She and Gideon were bundled under a thick robe. Becca had placed hot bricks on the floorboard to help keep them warm.

"Hold your horses, Annabeth. I need to find a bucket," he called from the inside of the shed, where he had parked his car when he first arrived.

"What do you need a bucket for?" Gideon shouted. "We are going caroling, not milking."

Tully came out of the shed holding a rusty pail in one hand. "I need a bucket, because that's the only way I can carry a tune."

Gideon threw back his head and laughed. "You are the funniest man. Is there anything you won't turn into a joke?"

Speaking to the bishop.

Tully put the bucket aside and got into the sleigh beside Becca. "You think I'm kidding. I cannot sing."

"The Lord only asks us to make joyful noise," she said dryly.

"Oh, I can do that."

"Make a joyful noise unto the Lord, all the earth: make a loud noise, and rejoice, and sing praise. Psalm ninety-eight, verse four," Gideon said. "Oh, come all ye faithful," he began in his rich baritone.

Annabeth and Becca joined in as she urged Cupcake to get moving. She nudged Tully with her elbow. He started singing but so softly. She nudged him again. He sat up straight and began to belt out the words.

She cringed. "Are you doing that on purpose?"

"You asked for it." He began the next verse with Annabeth and Gideon.

Becca laughed. "You do have a terrible singing voice.

Patricia Davids 199

Wait. You sang in the barn for Dotty. You weren't this bad."

"That was different. I didn't have an audience except for you and the cow, so it didn't matter."

"How flattering," she drawled.

"Flattery is not our way," he said, folding his arms over his chest.

"Our way?" she asked quietly.

"I'm glad you caught that. Here's hoping the bishop gives me a chance to make it the truth."

They traveled quickly through the snowy countryside to the Fisher home. A half dozen buggies and other sleighs were lined up beside the barn when they arrived.

Gabe stepped out of the barn and took hold of Cupcake's bridle. "I will take care of her. Go on into the house. I think everyone is here now."

Seth came out with Asher to help carry Gideon inside so he didn't have to struggle through the snow on his crutches. Becca allowed Tully to help her out of the sleigh. He held her hand as she stepped down. She looked up into his eyes. Could she see the love he had for her in their depths? A love that had to remain unspoken for now. Maybe forever. She looked down and pulled her hand away from him. He followed her inside.

The first thing that struck Tully as he entered the home of the Fisher family was the noise. The house was filled with happy chatter and laughter as Amish and *Englisch* friends waited for the start of the caroling. The warmth in the house had as much to do with the camaraderie among the occupants as with the roaring fire in the fireplace.

This was what he wanted for his life. This feeling of belonging to a group of people who truly cared for one another. He saw the bishop standing beside Gideon's chair and made his way over to him. "Bishop Schultz, may I have a moment of your time. Somewhere private?"

The bishop and Gideon exchanged pointed glances. Bishop Schultz nodded. "Come with me."

Tully followed him to one of the downstairs bedrooms. The bishop closed the door behind them. "What can I help you with?"

"I feel in my heart that I want to join your faith. I want to learn what I must do to become Amish."

"I assume Becca is the cause of this desire to become one of us?"

"I would be lying if I said she wasn't the reason I first thought about it. She has forbidden me to speak of my feelings until I have the right to address her."

"Very wise of her."

"But I want you to know there is more to my desire to know God than hoping Becca will one day be my wife. I have never felt as close to God as I do when I am among your people. I can't even say what it is that makes me feel that way. I have never met such caring folks."

"There are caring people everywhere. We are not that unique."

"You feel that this is a whim of mine."

"Is it?"

"No. Even if Becca refuses me, I want to live among you, worship as you do. Care for each other as you do. Am I making sense?"

"This is what I will say. You must live among us as one of us for a year. If after six months you still feel as you do now, I will allow you to take instructions. If you are unmoved in your determination at the end of the year, I will agree to baptize you. However, the entire church must agree, as well. You may spend a year with us and not be admitted. Are you prepared for that?"

A year with no guarantees. He didn't have a job or a place to live. If he did this, it was going to be on faith alone. Arnie was going to be shocked. Tully nodded. "I am."

"You will have to hang up your cowboy hat for good and wear proper Amish clothes. Including suspenders. I pray the Lord blesses your decision and your journey."

Tully wanted to shout for joy. He was being given a chance. He was eager to tell Becca, but it would have to wait until after they finished caroling and were alone again. He would tell her everything, about his addiction and his struggle to stay sober. He would start the relationship with a clean slate. Maybe then he could finally take her in his arms.

As he and the bishop left the bedroom, Tully looked for Becca but couldn't find her. He soon discovered she was already outside on the large sled the Fishers would use to carry them from house to house. She had Annabeth on her lap. Gideon was seated beside her. Tully didn't think he'd ever seen a more beautiful sight than Becca with her child on her lap under the stars, her face lit by the lanterns on the sides of the sleigh. She was everything he had ever wanted.

He looked for a place to sit near her and didn't see one.

"Over here, Cowboy," Gabe called out, waving him toward another, smaller sled. This one held only young men.

Tully climbed up with their help, and he was soon

surrounded with a boisterous bunch. He didn't realize until the sleighs began moving that he and Becca were going in different directions. He settled back to enjoy the night and the company. He would give Becca the news on their way home.

Becca had seen Tully leave the room with the bishop, but she had been ushered outside before he returned. She'd had only a glimpse of his face before they got underway without him. What had the bishop said to him?

"Smile, Becca, this is fun," Gemma said.

"Okay, I'm smiling." She kept the grin on her face for most of the next two hours as they traveled from house to house along the snow-covered road that led south out of New Covenant. It was fun. She and Annabeth sang until they were becoming hoarse. When Mr. Fisher finally brought them home, Annabeth was almost asleep on Becca's lap. She climbed in the back seat with her child in her arms and snuggled under a quilt. Gabe brought Tully's group in a few minutes later. He jumped off the sled and got up in front with Gideon, who then handed Tully the lines. He looked back at Becca. "I have something I need to tell you."

Annabeth sat up. "Are we home yet?"

Tully smiled at her. "Not yet, sleepyhead, but we will be soon." He spoke to Cupcake, and the big horse stepped forward eagerly. Out on the highway, they saw Gabe returning the empty sled. His horse was limping badly. He stopped and pulled over to the side of the road. Tully went past him and stopped a few feet in front. "Can I give you a hand?"

"No, thanks, Cowboy. I'll unhitch and take Chester home and come back with another horse."

Tully waved and went on his way. A few seconds later, a huge bang shattered the stillness of the night. Becca looked back. The wreckage of the sled was scattered across the road. A red car had spun off into the ditch.

It was so much like the scene of her husband's death that she got out of the sleigh and ran toward the wreckage, screaming, "Aaron! Aaron!"

Tully handed the lines to Gideon. "Who is Aaron?"

"Her husband. Go to her. I fear she is in shock."

Tully hopped down and ran to her. He grasped her by the shoulders and held her tight. "It's okay. Aaron isn't here."

She moaned and held on to him. He looked around and saw Gabe standing beside his horse a few dozen yards away. "Gabe, are you okay?"

"By the grace of God."

Tully held Becca away from him. "I have to go see about the driver."

She seemed to have regained her senses. "He may be hurt. Do you have your phone?"

"I don't."

It wasn't needed. A second car came along and stopped. That driver got out with his phone in hand. As they looked on, the door of the red car opened and a young man staggered out. He marched over to Tully. "Did you see what idiot left a wagon in the middle of my lane?"

He reeked of alcohol. Tully looked at Becca. Her eyes were wide with disbelief. "This isn't your lane. This is a highway, and that sled was on the shoulder. What's wrong with you?"

"It is too my lane. I live right over…" He spun in a wobbly circle and threw his arm to the left. "Over there."

It was an empty field. The second driver took the man's arm. "You're drunk, buddy. Come sit in my car till the cops get here."

"I'm not going to jail again," he muttered as he was led away.

"He's drunk! Just like the man that killed Aaron, his brother and his mother. How can they do it? How can they get in a car and disregard the life of everyone else? The man is disgusting." She pressed a hand to her head. "That's not right. I have to forgive him. I have to forgive them both."

Tully led her to the sleigh and helped her in. "Take her home, Gideon."

She grasped Tully's arm. "You said you had something to tell me."

He opened his mouth and closed it. What could he say in the face of her revulsion? She would look at him that way when he told her. He couldn't bear that.

"I'm leaving New Covenant. Tonight. You have been amazing people, but I can't give up my English life. Goodbye. I'll have someone take me to get my car and someone to help you with the chores."

He turned around and walked toward Gabe in a body that had gone numb.

Chapter Fifteen

"So you bailed on her. Instead of telling her the truth, you just took off with your tail between your legs and didn't look back."

Tully sat on the sofa in Arnie's small one-bedroom apartment in downtown Caribou. He had told his friend the entire story of his relationship with Becca and how he had no choice but to leave. He expected a little sympathy, but that was not what Arnie was dishing out. "You didn't see her face. You didn't see how upset she was."

"I knew you were a drunk, but I never knew you were a coward."

"I thought the two went hand in hand." That was exactly how he was feeling. Failure one and failure two.

"So you left the woman you love behind and you stopped for a drink or six on your way here."

Tully looked up. "No. I promise you, I haven't touched a drop."

"Why not? Sounds like you had a pretty good reason to me."

Tully rubbed his hands on his jeans. Even if he never

saw her again, Becca would always be his lodestone. The compass he used to guide the course of his life. He would never do anything to dishonor her memory. "Do I want a drink? Of course I do. Will I take a drink? No."

"Then I guess we have established that you are not a drunk."

"Just a coward. I knew what I would see in her eyes when I told her I was an alcoholic. I couldn't bear to see her turn away from me." Leaving was less painful than having her tell him to get out of her life.

"So what now?"

"I was hoping I could bunk with you for a while until I can get a job."

"That's a little bit of a plan. What kind of job?"

"I don't care. I don't care about much of anything anymore."

"You are lying to yourself, man. You do care. Not about what job to get, but about the people you ran out on. That little girl is going to be heartbroken if you don't go to her Christmas program."

Becca and Gideon would accept his leaving and understand that he didn't belong in their world, but how was a seven-year-old girl going to understand that he didn't want to stay with her anymore? "She'll get over it."

"Like you got over not having a mother and I got over a father that walked out on me when I was ten. Sure, she'll get over it, on the outside, just like we have, but what about on the inside? Do you think she's gonna feel that she wasn't good enough for you?"

Tully got to his feet. "I think coming here was a mistake."

Arnie held up one hand. "Don't go. I'm sorry. It's just

that when I talked to you last week, you were certain you had found what was missing in your life. You had found a woman who made you feel complete. A child who wanted you as her father. Even a community of people who made you feel welcome and valued. You found your way back to God. Do you know how many people never find half of what you had in your hands and tossed away?"

Tully raked his hands through his hair. He wasn't a good enough man for Becca. She would see that. "I can't change what I am."

"Really? Because you used to be a stumbling drunk living out of his car in a run-down neighborhood where even the rats thought twice about taking up residence. I think you've changed a lot."

"On the outside."

"No, Cowboy, you've changed on the inside. What is the one thing you wanted when you got out of rehab?"

"A drink."

"Oh, funny, ha-ha. What did you tell me when I asked if you were looking for a job?"

"I don't remember."

"You said you just needed to find one person to have faith in you and believe you would stay sober."

"Okay, I may have said that."

Arnie rose to his feet and put a hand on Tully's shoulder. "How can you ask others to have faith in you when you refuse to have faith in them? Let me rephrase that. When you refuse to have faith in her."

Tully had no answer for him.

"You couldn't take a chance that she would reject you. You would've been crushed, I get that. You would've been miserable. You know what I see?"

"Don't hold back, tell me what you really think."

"You're still crushed and miserable. How is this any better? It's late. I'm going to bed. The couch is yours. I would say sleep well, but I suspect you won't. And just so you know, if you don't go back to her, you're a whopping fool."

Tully sat down on the sofa after Arnie left the room. What did Arnie know? He didn't have a drinking problem. He didn't know what it was like to have people look down their noses at him. To know they were judging him and finding him less of a man.

He pulled his boots off and stretched out with his arms behind his head. Sleep was the furthest thing from his mind. He kept seeing the tears that had glistened in Becca's beautiful eyes when he told her he was leaving.

He wanted to believe that she could accept the flawed man that he was, but what if she couldn't? What if she turned away from him? What if he saw disgust in her eyes instead of tears? How could he bear it if every time she looked at him, she saw the man that killed her husband?

If he didn't have faith in her, how could he expect her to have faith in him? He did have faith in her. It was himself he doubted.

What's the plan, God? I'm lost. I'm tired. I thought I knew what I wanted, but what do You want from me?

Through the thin walls of Arnie's apartment, he heard Christmas music playing, or maybe it was coming from outside. He got up, went to the window and pulled the curtain aside. The streets of the city were decorated with lights and giant ornaments. There was a Christmas tree in the courtyard below. A group of carolers stood around it singing "Silent Night."

Tomorrow night Annabeth and her classmates would be singing the same song for their family and friends, and he wouldn't be there to hear it.

The song ended, and a man's voice began a new hymn. "Love came down at Christmas, love all lovely, love divine, love was born at Christmas, star and angels gave the sign."

Tully let the curtain fall back and returned to the couch. He sat with his elbows propped on his knees and his head in his hands.

If you don't go back to her, you're a whopping fool.

Arnie's words echoed through Tully's mind. *How is this any better?*

It wasn't. It never would be. Life without Becca, Annabeth, Gideon and all the people of New Covenant would only be half a life. Hadn't he already lost enough of himself to his alcoholism? Did he have to lose the rest to his fears? There was no place left to run and hide unless he went back into a bottle, and he would not do that.

Somewhere in the back of his mind, he would always wonder what Becca would have said if he had told her the truth. Knowing had to be better than never knowing. His hands grew icy as he faced what he had to do.

Tomorrow he would go back. If he was going to lose Becca, it would have to be her choice. If he hadn't lost her already.

"*Mamm*, where is my shepherd's crook?" Annabeth hollered from her room.

"It's here in the kitchen by the front door where you put it so you wouldn't forget it."

Annabeth came running into the room. She grabbed

up the crook Gideon had made for her. "I'm ready. Is it time to go yet?"

"Not yet. We have an hour before you're supposed to be there."

"Do you think Tully will change his mind and come see me?"

Becca's chest contracted with pain. Why couldn't he have waited until after Christmas? It would've been easier for Annabeth, but not for her. She had tried to prepare herself for the inevitable, but it hadn't done any good. After thinking she would never love another, Tully—an *Englischer* and beyond her reach unless she was willing to forsake her faith—had proven her wrong. Her heart was in tatters.

"I hear a car! It's Tully, I know it is." Annabeth raced to look out the window.

Becca felt her heart leap and then drop. She couldn't get her hopes up.

Annabeth turned away from the window with tears glistening in her eyes. Her lower lip quivered. "It's not his car." She ran down the hall to her room and closed the door.

Becca forced herself to go see who it was. She opened the door and looked out. It was a small white pickup. She didn't recognize the man behind the steering wheel, but she saw an Amish fellow get out of the passenger seat. He leaned down and spoke to the driver, who then pulled away, leaving the man standing a few paces beyond her gate. In the same spot where she had first seen Tully holding an injured newborn calf. The memory brought tears to her eyes.

The man walked closer. She blinked back her tears when she realized it was Tully. She held on to the door to keep upright. Or maybe so she wouldn't race down the steps and throw herself into his arms. Why was he here? Why was he dressed like an Amish fellow instead of like a cowboy? Where did he get the clothes?

She heard Gideon and Annabeth talking as they came down the hall. She grabbed her coat and turned to them as they entered the kitchen. "I'm going to check on Diamond before we leave."

She stepped out, closed the door behind her and pointed to the barn. She marched past him without speaking. Whatever his reason was for being here, she didn't want him to upset Annabeth and Gideon if they happened to look out and catch sight of him. She hardened her resolve against the turmoil seeing him again caused. He had vanished with barely a word of goodbye, leaving her and her child brokenhearted. If he could do it once, he could do it again. Only this time she would be prepared.

Inside the barn she lit a lamp and braced herself as she turned to face him with her arms clasped tightly across her chest. She looked his clothing up and down. "What is this? Some new show like your rope tricks?"

"Hello, Becca." He took off his hat and started turning it in his hands. "Michael supplied me with a proper outfit."

Tears sprang to her eyes at the tenderness in his voice. She turned away and braced her arms on the gate of Diamond's stall. "What are you doing here?"

"I'm taking the biggest risk of my life."

"What is that supposed to mean?" Her voice broke on the last word, and she struggled to breathe against the tightness in her throat.

He stepped up beside her, leaning on the gate, too.

Diamond hobbled over to nuzzle his knee through the wooden slats. He scratched her head. "It means I have something to tell you, but I am scared to death to open my mouth."

Her hands were shaking, but she managed to clasp them tightly together. Her fingers were like ice. "Do you think coming dressed as one of us will make what you have to say more acceptable to me? Clothing has nothing to do with belonging here. You said it yourself. You couldn't give up your English ways."

"I was lying about that."

Shocked, she turned to face him. "Why would you lie to me?"

"Because I thought that lie would be less painful than the truth about me. I know that I hurt you, and I'm deeply sorry. You may not believe it, but I was trying to protect you. No, that isn't the whole truth. I was trying to protect myself."

She still couldn't make sense of what he was saying. "What is this terrible truth that made you leave and now makes you come back?" Did he know he was breaking her heart all over again?

"Becca… I am an alcoholic. Just like the man who ran a stop sign and killed your husband, your brother-in-law and Gideon's wife. Just like the man we saw staggering away from the wreckage of Gabe's sled."

"I can't believe that." Of all the things she had expected to hear, this was not one of them.

"I should've told you before you let me stay with you and your family. You had a right to know the kind of man that was living in your home."

This was the secret she had seen in his eyes. The thing he'd kept from her. She tried to hold down the anger rising inside her. What did knowing this change? He'd found it easier to walk away from her love than to trust her.

He cleared his throat. "I hope you can forgive me."

Part of her wanted to throw her arms around him and tell him it was okay. The other part of her wanted to scream, *why?* What hold did alcohol have over him that was more powerful than a family's love or the value of a human life?

As she looked at his tense, pale features, her anger drained away. Her heart filled with pity. "I'm sorry you have this burden to bear. You have told me. Is that all?"

"Except to say that I'm sorry for the hurt that I have caused you and that people like me have caused you. I was plastered when I let a friend drive drunk. He killed himself and two other people."

"You are not responsible for the sins of others. You are not the man who took my husband's life."

"Thank you." He put his hat on his head. "I guess that's it." He started to walk away.

She couldn't let him go with so much unsaid. "What do you plan to do now?"

"I turned in my Stetson for a flat-topped black Amish hat, and I sold my car. I will find an Amish community and live as they do. In time I hope to bury my *Englisch* past completely. I want to thank you for showing me the way to a place where I think God wants me to belong."

She swallowed hard against the faint hope that started to rise from the depths of her pain. "Why can't you stay among us? Did the bishop disapprove?"

His smile was sad. "No, but it would be too hard to live near you and not be a part of your life. I know I would be a constant reminder of your husband's untimely death. I care about you too much to subject you to that."

He cared enough to leave, but did he care enough to stay? "When you were here with us, were you drinking?"

"No. I had been out of rehab for only a few months when I bumped into Diamond on the road. I have not had a drink since I went into rehab. I have been sober for five months. I know that doesn't sound like much to you, but for me it's huge. I had planned to tell you that night, but after learning how your husband died, I got scared. I didn't want you to look at me the way you looked at that man, so I left."

"You have given up drinking?"

"Yup. I know it will be a lifelong struggle, but I can't go back to what I was. You helped me see that—among other things."

She took a step toward him. Something in his voice told her she hadn't heard the whole truth yet. "What other things?"

A tiny smile pulled at the corner of his mouth. "That kindness exists. That a house can be a real home if the people in it care about each other. That a community can love and nurture all its members. That God loves me and has a plan for me." He looked into her eyes. "I had stopped believing before I met you."

He was in love with her, and he was about to walk away again. She saw it in the depths of despair in his eyes. Why couldn't he tell her? Was he afraid she would cast his love aside? Had she given him a reason to think otherwise? "You have shown me something important, too, Tully Lange."

He looked away. "How to spin a rope?"

"*Nee*, you will not distract me with your humor. You will listen to what I have to tell you. The rules of my faith control every part of my life, from what I wear on my head to what prayers I say at night. Despite knowing it was wrong and trying very hard not to do so…I still fell in love with you."

Tully's gaze flew to her face—he wasn't sure that he had heard correctly. His heart began hammering in his chest. He was afraid he was dreaming. "What did you say?"

"I think you heard me."

"Maybe I did, but I would sure like to hear you say that again."

"I said I'm in love with you. Even if it doesn't make a difference, I wanted you to know."

He took a step toward her. "That is the most beautiful thing I have ever heard in my life. Spoken by the most beautiful woman I've ever seen. The dairy barn setting isn't so spectacular, but I can live with it. As long as you mean it."

A smile curved her lips. "We have spent so much time together in this barn that it seemed like the perfect setting."

He had never known such joy. "Becca, I love you. If you don't mind, I'd like to spend the next sixty or seventy years working beside you in this barn." He held out his arms. When she stepped into his embrace, he knew he had found his own paradise.

He held her close as tears of happiness slipped down his cheeks. "I thought I had lost you. I thought you'd never be able to look at me again when you knew what I was."

She gazed up at him and cupped his cheeks with her hands. "I always knew you were a cowboy, and I love you in spite of it."

"I'm the one that makes the jokes."

"I am not joking. Why couldn't you tell me that you loved me just now?"

"Because I didn't believe that I deserved to have something so wonderful in my life." He pulled her into a fierce hug. "I still don't deserve you, but I'm never going to let you go."

"Oh, Tully, I love you so much. I can't believe how happy I am, but if you are going to kiss me you had better do it now, because we have to get Annabeth to her Christmas program."

"I love the way you boss me around." He bent toward her upturned face and tenderly pressed his lips to hers.

The outside door banged open, and Annabeth came in. "*Mamm*, we are going to be late! Tully!" She threw herself into his arms. "I knew you would come. I knew it."

"I wouldn't miss your play for anything." He held out his hand to Becca. "Shall we go?"

"With you? Everywhere and for always."

"It will be a year before I can be baptized."

"Then the wedding will be in one year and one day."

He tipped his head to the side. "Did you just propose to me?"

"I did. You were dragging your feet."

"I accept."

"*Goot.*" She made shooing motions with her hands. "Let's go. We have to celebrate Christmas with our friends and family."

Tully lifted Annabeth up and set her on his shoulder.

"And some little shepherd girl has to find the Christ child."

"We are blessed, Tully Lange," Becca said stepping to his side.

He dropped a quick kiss on her lips. "Don't I know it."

Annabeth squeaked. "Did you just kiss my mother?"

"Yup. Want to see me do it again?"

She grinned. "Yup."

* * * * *

If you enjoyed this story,
look for these other books
by Patricia Davids:

Dear Reader,

Welcome back to New Covenant, Maine. I hope you have enjoyed your visit to this remarkable community. Every time I start writing about them, they surprise me with some new facet of their faith.

My hero, Tully, struggled with addiction. I have never faced that challenge, but I know people who have. I'm sure most of us can say that. It is not my intention to make light of the issue with this story. Nor do I mean to imply that the problem is specific to those who have served our country. I would never belittle the cost of their sacrifices in such a trivial fashion. I wish to thank all of them for their service.

As for an outsider joining the Amish faith, it is enjoyable to write such a story, but in reality it rarely happens. My hat is off to anyone who can make that leap. I couldn't. The three times my power went out due to the weather while I was writing this story were totally frustrating. I need my computer.

I prefer to believe as many Amish do that God allows all men to seek Him in their own ways. My way may not be your way, but neither of us is wrong if our hearts are open to His will.

Enjoy the Lord's many blessings at this wonderful time of year. Merry Christmas and happy New Year to you and all those you love.

Patricia Davids

WE HOPE YOU ENJOYED
THIS BOOK FROM

LOVE INSPIRED
INSPIRATIONAL ROMANCE

Uplifting stories of faith, forgiveness and hope.

Fall in love with stories where faith helps
guide you through life's challenges, and discover
the promise of a new beginning.

6 NEW BOOKS AVAILABLE EVERY MONTH!

Don't miss the third book in
The Off Season series by *USA TODAY* bestselling author

LEE TOBIN McCLAIN

There's no better place to spend Christmas than on the Chesapeake Bay, where it's always the perfect season to start over.

"It's emotional, tender, and an all-around wonderful story."
—RaeAnne Thayne, *New York Times* bestselling author, on *Low Country Hero*

Order your copy today!

HQNBooks.com

PHLTMBPA1020

SPECIAL EXCERPT FROM

This holiday season, Amber Rowe is taken by surprise when Paul Thompson moves into the cottage next door with his young son. Falling for the single dad is risky for so many reasons, but the magic of their Chesapeake Bay town at Christmas might just bring them together...

Read on for a peek at
Christmas on the Coast, *the next emotional and heartwarming book in* USA TODAY *bestselling author Lee Tobin McClain's The Off Season series!*

"When are we going to decorate cookies?" Davey asked. Clearly, he'd gotten bored with the gift-wrapping discussion.

"Just give me five minutes, buddy," Amber said. "What color frosting do you think would look best on the gingerbread boys?"

"All the colors!" Davey waved his hands wide. "'Specially blue. That's my favorite."

"Well, okay, then." Amber pulled up the white frosting she'd made before, quickly divided it into smaller bowls, and found her food coloring. She hummed as she stirred it in, creating a rainbow of frosting colors, with Davey kneeling on a chair beside her, giving advice. All the while, she kept putting in new trays of gingerbread cookies to bake, setting up an assembly line.

Quickly, she got both Davey and Paul set up with frosting and gingerbread boys. "You decorate these however you want to," she said. "I trust your judgment."

"That might be a mistake," Paul said, but he gamely scooped up a lump of pink frosting and spread it over one of the cookies. Davey watched, then did the same with blue frosting.

PHLTMEXP1020

Amber found some colored sugar and other decorations that she and Hannah had used to make cookies in years past, and she pulled out a bunch of them for the boys to use. Sarge ran around devouring bits of cookie and frosting that fell to the floor.

"We're decorating cookies in school," Davey said, his tongue poking out the corner of his mouth as he concentrated on his work. "Miss Kayla said I was good at it. Now I'll be even better."

"Miss Kayla is smart," Amber commented, letting her gaze flicker to Paul's. She was pretty sure she didn't have anything to worry about in terms of Kayla, from what Paul had said before, but she couldn't restrain a slight feeling of jealousy.

"She's very understanding," Paul said, raising his eyebrows at Amber. "She can read between the lines. I'll have to tell you about that some time."

"She's a good reader," Davey agreed. He squirted a huge glob of yellow frosting onto the head of a gingerbread boy.

Amber had to laugh at the double conversation that was going on, and Paul's lips twitched, as well.

She loved sharing a joke with him. Loved sharing holiday preparations and memories with him. The air was full of the smell of cookies, along with the pine scent of the little Christmas tree she'd bought. Christmas carols hummed away on the radio.

If only this could go on. Maybe it could go on. But not if secrets stood between them.

Certainty came to her: if she wanted this to go on, she needed to tell Paul the truth, and sooner rather than later.

Don't miss Lee Tobin McClain's
Christmas on the Coast,
available now from HQN Books!

HQNBooks.com